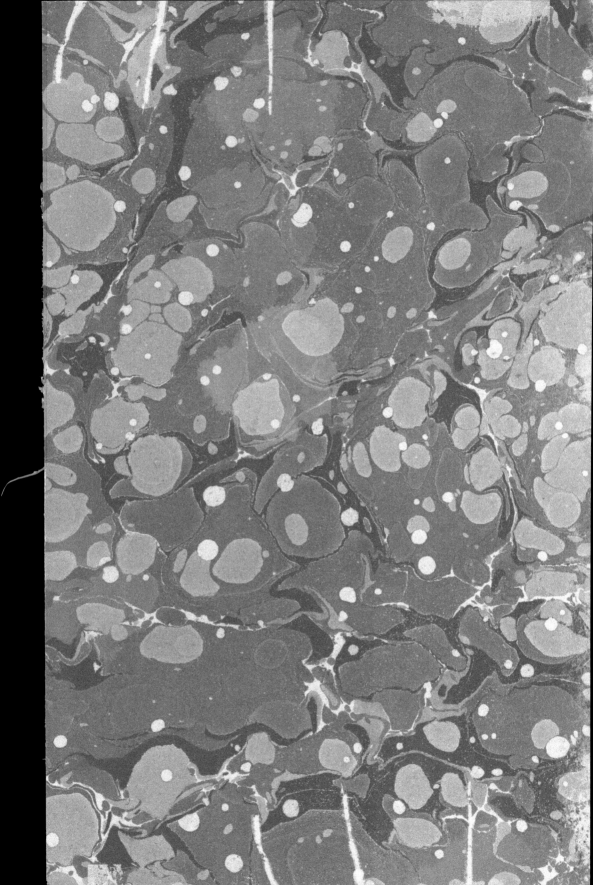

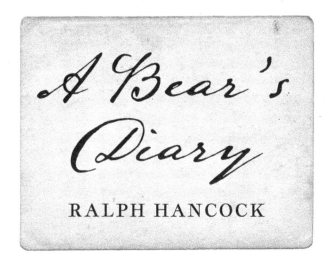

A Bear's Diary

RALPH HANCOCK

Matador
9 Priory Business Park,
Wistow Road, Kibworth Beauchamp,
Leicestershire. LE8 0RX
Tel: 0116 279 2299
Email: books@troubador.co.uk
Web: www.troubador.co.uk/matador
Twitter: @matadorbooks

ISBN 978 1838594 626

British Library Cataloguing in Publication Data.
A catalogue record for this book is available from the British Library.

Printed and bound by CPI Group (UK) Ltd, Croydon, CR0 4YY
Typeset in 11pt Orthos by Troubador Publishing Ltd, Leicester, UK

Matador is an imprint of Troubador Publishing Ltd

To all the Puffins

1.

Cambridge, November 6th, 1805.

I did not dance well at the Bonfire Night show on Midsummer Common. Afterwards, Fred said to me, 'Daisy, me ole dear. Yer knows and I knows yer gettin' a bit old for this game. An' I got Bruin, an' 'e's learnin' fast. 'E's a chip orf the ole block. Now, Daisy, yer bin a good bear an' a good friend to me all these years, an' I'll not see yer starve, I'll do right by yer.

There's this lord, Byron 'e's called, 'e's a student at the university, an' 'e wants to buy yer. 'E says 'e ain't allowed to keep a dawg in 'is rooms, but there's nothin' in the rules agin 'avin' a bear. We 'ad a laugh about that. 'E seems a good enough lad, and I think yer'll be all right. Good lookin' boy, though 'e's a mite lame, gave me good money for yer. 'E's comin' to get yer tomorrer.'

My mind is all of a turmoil. It has been a good life with Fred, and we have had twelve European dance tours to great acclaim. But what he says is true. I am getting old, as happens to the best of dancing bears, and it is time to settle down. My dear cub Bruin – now two years old, how time passes! – will serve him well. And as for this young lord, we shall see. If he puts a foot wrong, he shall feel my powerful paw and my terrible teeth.

November 7th, 1805.

I am now a Lord's bear. He is only a Baron – George Gordon, Lord Byron – but I am not a snob about such matters. His friends call him George, and so shall I in this diary.

He came to collect me in a chaise, which showed a certain style. He is quite handsome for a human, with dark brown curly hair, but as Fred said he is lame. There is something wrong with his right foot, which he tries to disguise – as a bear I can well understand that, one must never show weakness.

He has found me a private room in a tower above his own quarters, with a comfortable bed of straw where I can lie at my ease. I have never enjoyed the luxury of a room of my own, but it is a little lonely there.

I had a good dinner with plenty of meat which was perhaps a little over-mature, but we bears are not fussy about such things. He also gave me a large pot of beer. Then we went out for a ramble on what he

called 'the Backs', a wild garden on the other side of the river from the buildings. Feeling jovial from the beer, and having a corner still left to fill, I caught a cat and ate it. George laughed. He said it was the Master's cat, but no one would know. Cats disappear the whole time.

On the way back to his rooms, I felt the need to – how shall I say? – answer Nature's call. This office I performed in a wide paved space which George said was called the Great Court. He also said that they would think it was the Bursar that had done it. This was probably no more than a jest, but who knows in this strange place?

I like George, but I miss my dear Fred.

November 10th, 1805.

George came home this evening shockingly inebriated, with a trollop on his arm. He opened a bottle of port and they shared it before they lurched off to bed together. My lord seems to be able to perform despite being more than three sheets to the wind. Good for him. But it was not a seemly spectacle and I retired to my room in the tower to ponder matters that only bears can understand.

December 2nd, 1805.

I am now well settled into life at Trinity College. George brings me plenty of food, not of the best quality but enough to keep a bear fighting fit. He explained to me that undergraduates are obliged to eat a certain number of dinners in the dining hall each term, but that the food is so disgusting that most of them pay for their dinners as they must but eat in nearby alehouses, so that much food is left over. He sends his manservant to the kitchen and pays the cooks a small amount for the uneaten meat, which he brings to me. I have just disposed of a good deal of what he said was chicken, but the meat is dark grey and I think it is crow. I have had worse and am not disposed to complain.

I spend my days in George's room, and at night retire to my private chamber. Long ago, Sir Isaac Newton had an observatory on the floor above me, and I like to fancy that he spent many hours looking through his telescope at the Great Bear and wondering whether those distant suns also had planets.

December 8th, 1805.

George was sadly intoxicated again last night. He had an essay to present to his tutor tomorrow, on Ammianus Marcellinus. I looked at his brief and feeble scrawls, and it was plain that they would not do. While he snored, I relit the candle and sat in his chair to write a proper essay for him.

I well remember my visit to Arbon in the Swiss Canton of Appenzell with Fred two years ago. In Roman times this was called Felix Arbor, and old Ammianus – one of my favourite writers – visited it in the autumn of the year 355. He made the curious observation that the Rhine flows into Lake Constance without mixing with the water of the lake, and bores through the lake to flow out at the other end as if it were enclosed in a pipe. Even a bear can understand that this is nonsense. But, standing in the ruins of the old Roman watchtower, now in a churchyard, and looking east from the promontory, I could see how he came by this idea. The river, swollen and muddy with autumn rains, flowed into the lake with great force and left a straight brown track stretching across the blue lake as far as the eye could see.

This I described as well as I could in my essay. When the low winter sun reluctantly crawled above the horizon the following morning, I awakened George – a sadly long business involving much groaning and not a little puking – and pushed him over to his desk to see what I had done. He was astonished and grateful, and hugged me warmly. I made him eat a breakfast of cold mutton washed down with small beer before he limped off pale-faced and unsteady to his tutor, clutching my work. My handwriting is not good, but it is better than his.

The manservant cleaned the floor. Rather him than me.

December 9th, 1805.

George told me that his tutor was mightily pleased by the essay on Ammianus that I had written for him, but had asked how it was that he had seen the Rhine. Luckily George had the presence of mind to stammer out that he had heard it from a friend who had been on the Grand Tour. I think that perhaps the two of us will get him through his course of studies, but it is the bear who will have to bear the burden, as bears do.

January 25th, 1806.

Yesterday evening George returned to his rooms with a boy from the chapel choir, one John Edleston. He plied the lad with Madeira, too strong a tipple in my view for one of such tender years. I will draw a veil over what followed, but suffice it to say that in the Navy such acts may get a man hanged. I flatter myself that, in my travels, I have seen the best and the worst of human conduct, but must confess that I was appalled by the spectacle and retired hastily to my room in the tower. I do have to admit that young John seemed quite cheerful when he left the following morning. Perhaps he is used to such treatment.

February 16th, 1806.

George has been writing poetry. While he was out roistering with his friends I cast an eye over his effusions, and I confess that I am not greatly impressed. Here are two stanzas from one of his poems.

> *The man, doom'd to sail*
> *With the blast of the gale,*
> *Through billows Atlantic to steer,*
> *As he bends o'er the wave*
> *Which may soon be his grave,*
> *The green sparkles bright with a Tear.*
>
> *The Soldier braves death*
> *For a fanciful wreath*
> *In Glory's romantic career;*
> *But he raises the foe*
> *When in battle laid low,*
> *And bathes every wound with a Tear.*

Well, I have been aboard a ship in an Atlantic gale and, believe me, the sailors were far too occupied to weep. And I was at the Battle of Marengo, and saw how the victorious French simply skewered their wounded enemies, and laughed as they did so.

George is only young, and if he keeps at it he may yet be a better poet. But I wish he would pay more attention to his studies. I have another essay to write for him this evening, on Xenophon's Anabasis.

February 17th, 1806.

My essay turned out well, and George returned smiling from his tutor's room and shook me warmly by the paw. I am getting the knack of writing these pieces.

I commented on the passage in which Xenophon's men are laid low by wild honey that they have gathered. We bears know that honey made from the flowers of the rhododendron is poisonous, and can instantly identify it by its odour, but humans' sense of smell is so poor that such discrimination is beyond them. Also, of course, Xenophon would not have been acquainted with this Asian shrub.

George's tutor had not known what had affected the honey, and was surprised by this revelation. The rhododendron has now been brought to this country, so when the tutor asked George how he knew the cause of the poisoning, he was able to mutter vaguely that it had happened to a friend of his who kept bees and had rhododendron bushes in his garden. Since no other explanation seemed possible, this flimsy story had to be accepted.

June 2nd, 1806.

A visit from George's stepsister Augusta Leigh. I am sorry to report that their relations are very far from those that one would expect from brother and sister. Not to put too fine a point on it, they spent the night in the same bed. Deeply shocked, I retired early to my private chamber.

The proctor's cat tells me that this is the sort of behaviour one must expect from the aristocracy, and related some appalling tales which modesty prevents me from setting down here.

2.

George is off to Italy, where I am sure he will have a capital time ogling churches and whores, and buying paintings that might be by Salvator Rosa but are probably not. I have made the Grand Tour; it is something that every young bear or man should do once, but only once. There was a bear in Florence – but I digress.

He has left me in the care of his manservant Jem Voakes, a good fellow and we are easy together. Jem is out of countenance because his lordship has not seen fit to pay him for three months, but he does not yet see the need to 'mizzle', as he puts it.

We went to a dogfight. I dislike these human pastimes. If I need to fight I will, but it is not an entertainment. Jem bet on the wrong dog and lost £2. He was mightily displeased.

Jem plays the flute well enough, and I indicated to him that he should strike up a tune. I danced – I cannot say that I did it well, as I am out of form and my old joints are stiff, but it was good enough for a dogfight crowd. We took requests for popular tunes, and made £8 2s 4¼d, though that last farthing was a brass one. Jem was much cheered and said I was a 'diamond bear'.

We went to the inn and drank porter. The owner of the losing dog was there, and the poor creature was in a bad way and not long for this world. I looked at the owner, and he took my meaning and nodded. I carried the dog outside, finished him quickly and ate most of him –

he was a big dog and I had to leave the foxes their portion. We bears understand simple folk better than we do the pampered nobles.

June 25th, 1807.

George has returned from his travels. I was glad to see him, but I must admit that I have enjoyed my time with Jem and his cronies more than watching him mollock with doxies and catamites in his chambers while I pen his essays on Aristotle and Plato. He has published his poems under the title of *Hours of Idleness*, and I must admit that it is a fitting title. The book contains many of the 'Fugitive Pieces' that he circulated among his friends, but he has omitted some of the more salacious odes and put in some new works. I cannot but think that those he removed were better and truer than the dull stuff he added.

The reviewers have not been kind, and he is downcast. We went for a ramble to Grantchester and both got royally drunk on the strong ale they serve at the Green Man. As we staggered back to Cambridge I happened on a badger, which I ate to George's amusement. I offered him some, but humans are oddly squeamish about such things. Notwithstanding that, he is happier now and inclined to accept his misfortunes philosophically, though I think he will have a sore head in the morning.

October 16th, 1806.

George has a new friend by the name of John Hobhouse, whom he refers to as 'Hobby'. To his other cronies he describes their relations as 'pure'. I have reason to think otherwise, but let it pass.

Meanwhile my time is more than occupied by writing essays on Homer and Hesiod, Sallust and Suetonius. To this end I have often visited the library attached to the college, a noble building designed by Sir Christopher Wren. I had some trepidation about gaining entry to this hallowed place, but I found that all that was necessary was to wear George's academic gown. The aged and purblind don who presides over the library is so eager to ensure that all entrants are properly attired that he is quite oblivious of their species, and I can wander among the deliciously musty bookcases to my heart's content.

December 19th, 1806.

I am concerned about George. Last night he lost £60 and a gold ring at faro. He has been playing deeper and deeper to recoup his losses, but he has never had either skill or luck at the tables. When he arrived in Cambridge with an income of £500 a year, it seemed that this was more than sufficient for a young nobleman to live handsomely, but he has squandered it in dissolute living. Two wine merchants and three tailors have already refused to extend any further credit to him, and I have noticed that the trollops he brings to his rooms are coarser than before. This morning he lit the fire with his bootmaker's bill, which was not a small one as he has special boots made to conceal the deformity of his right foot.

So far his charm has carried him through, but I am fearful of what the future may bring.

April 20ᵗʰ, 1808.

George's final examinations are rapidly approaching. He has done no work whatever, and has merely spent the time roistering with his friends and sundry loose women and looser boys. It is clear that he is in no state to attend these crucial trials, and that I shall have to impersonate him. My experience at the library suggests that I shall be able to carry it off.

Jem will ensure that he is plied with sufficient drink on the eve of each paper to prevent him from rising before noon, and will lock the door of his rooms to prevent him from wandering about during the hours set for each paper. What he does during the evening is of no importance, though the other students will be spending long and anxious candlelit hours revising their knowledge. I have no need of this: I have not wasted the last three years. (Well, not much of them – George and Jem and I have had many a roaring time, of which I have fond memories.)

May 4ᵗʰ, 1808.

The examinations have begun. I was much amused by the ease with which I was able to take my lord Byron's desk, merely by donning the required garb. It is true that the dons have not seen much of him during his residence at Trinity.

Nevertheless, it is a punishing time. There are two papers of three hours every day. My paw aches from having to grasp a quill designed for human hands for so long, and my mental powers are on the verge of exhaustion. Today I had to write a Latin version of Gray's Elegy in hexameter metre, and I flatter myself that I did not give a bad account of it, though my rustic Latin is a long way down the stream of time from the pure source of Virgil:

Vespertina notat finem campana diei,
pigra armenta boant, tarde tenduntque per agros;
passibus erga domum lassis se vertit arator,
et totas terras tenebrisque mihique relinquit.

I will not trouble you with the rest of my attempt. I must admit that I would rather dance in chains for a fortnight than undergo this protracted inquisition, but I feel kindly towards George, who may be an idle fellow but has treated me well, and I will do my best to help him.

May 10th, 1808.

I was delighted to see that one of the questions was on Tacitus' account of the defeat of Boudicca (or Boadicea if you will, but that name is from a corrupt medieval manuscript), a topic perhaps not unexpected in an examination set by an English university. Some years ago I danced in the Bullring in Birmingham, and between performances Fred and I rambled around the outer reaches of this sooty town. No one knows where the final battle took place, except that it was a long way from the homeland of Boudicca's tribe, the Iceni, in Norfolk. Our wanderings took us south to Stirchley, a humble village near King's Norton whose main street, straight as an arrow, gives a clear indication that the Romans were here, and indeed it was the main road between Letocetum (now Well) and Salinae (now Droitwich).

The road runs at a slight elevation above the banks of the Rea, a small but ill-tempered river which, when swollen by rain, often floods an extensive area of the valley, which at other times is a treacherous marsh. A bare two miles to the north, in the even more miserable village of

Metchley, lie the remains of a Roman military encampment. We observed (or it would be fairer to say that I observed, as Fred is no historian) that there is another road that runs parallel to the Roman one behind the crest of the low hills to the east of the valley, and along which a whole legion could pass unobserved from below, then suddenly descend into the valley and annihilate an ill-armed band whose war chariots were bogged down in the marsh, as Tacitus suggests.

This is only a fancy of mine, but it is a topic to win the attention of an examiner, and I hope it has had that effect.

May 20th, 1808.

I sat the last paper this afternoon, and am very happy to write that the imposture has been a complete success. Not an eyebrow has been raised as I entered and left the examination room, draped in my voluminous gown. George, who I must admit was, as usual, pretty far gone on inferior port by this time of day, embraced me tearfully and said that I was a bear beyond compare, and he would write a heroic ode to me in the style of Pindar. 'In English, of course,' he hastily added. I do not think the Greek ode I wrote in the examination was very good, but George could not have composed the first line.

We celebrated my achievement at a local alehouse. I had to carry George home, not for the first time. The faithful Jem helped me to put him to bed.

Now we shall have to wait a fortnight for the results to be posted.

June 2nd, 1808.

I have won a First! – or properly I should say that George has got it, and his name is on the list which was posted on the noticeboard this afternoon. Yet we know who laboured for it, and the honour is mine. Unknown to the world at large I am a Bachelor of Arts, a strange distinction for a matron, not to mention a bear.

George and Jem were as delighted as I, and we danced around Great Court until my acute eye detected a proctor emerging from the

gatehouse. Luckily we were in the opposite corner and were able to leave by the screens passage past the entrance to the Hall and into Nevile's Court, and across the river to the Backs. From thence, of course, it seemed natural to continue to an inn, where we toasted our success in what the landlord described as claret. After a dinner of tolerable roast

mutton we continued our celebrations until long after midnight, the hour when the college gate is locked.

There is a fairly easy climb in over a wall to the left of the gate, with a tree growing conveniently near to aid the ascent. Nevertheless, it was only with some effort that we were able to haul up an inert George, with Jem pulling from the top of the wall and me pushing from below. The street was still loud with undergraduates shouting of their success or bewailing their failure, and we reached George's rooms without incident.

When he was snoring stertorously in his bed, Jem said to me, 'Daisy, there's summat I needs to tell yer. Yer done right by George, and I done right by 'im, an' 'e's well settled now. But 'e ain't paid me for more 'n a year, and I'm considerin' movin' on. An' I don't see what 'e'll do wiv yer when 'e comes down from university, an' that's not long now.

'But I got a plan. Like 'is lordship says, yer a bear o' great brain, and I think you an' me's got a future together. I was thinkin', we could set up a dancin' school for bears, take in young cubs an' train 'em up an' send 'em out to earn a good livin' like yer done yerself. I even thought o' a name for it, The Bear Necessities. Think about it, Daisy me gal. There's no 'urry for a while. We got to get George presentable-like in the mornin' anyways.'

June 3rd, 1808.

After a sleepless night in my room in the tower, not aided by the consequences of the execrable wine, I have decided that Jem's plan is a sound one. We have guided George along his stormy course for long enough. He is a published poet, for what that is worth, and it is time that he stood on his own two feet, twisted as they may be.

We leave tonight. There will be no farewells. But I shall leave a copy of this journal on George's desk, and perhaps he will understand our reasons for departure, though more likely he will not. I wish him every success.

3.

I take up my pen again in London, where Jem and I have arrived after our hasty departure from Cambridge. It is quite understandable that Jem, unpaid by his lordship for more than a year, has made amends by relieving him of his silverware, and we have paid for food and lodging on our journey a spoon at a time.

At Baldock we happened on my old master Fred, who was passing through with a band of travelling performers, and I was joyfully reunited with my cub Bruin, now a seasoned dancer who varies his routines with impressions of well known public figures. His impersonation of His Royal Highness The Prince of Wales had us all in stitches, and earned us £4 11s 7d when we took up a collection from the patrons of the inn where we were staying.

Fred was much taken by Jem's notion of setting up an academy for dancing bears. 'There's bears and there's bears,' he said. 'Now Bruin's an *artiste*' – he pronounced the word with careful respect – 'and Daisy, in yer prime there was no one like yer. But on my travels I seen some bear acts that fair made me blub, they was so bad. Dancin's an art and gotta be learnt proper.'

He decided to come to London with us, and of course with dear Bruin. His large acquaintance will be to our advantage in finding us pupils.

Fred also has friends in London, and after a little consultation he has found us premises in a former stable to the west of the city between the

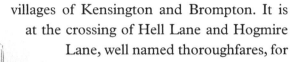

villages of Kensington and Brompton. It is at the crossing of Hell Lane and Hogmire Lane, well named thoroughfares, for it stands in a district of market gardens where fruit and vegetables are grown for sale in the metropolis. These are manured with what is politely called 'night soil', that is to say human excrement dredged from the city's innumerable cesspits and transported here daily in carts. The stink is overpowering, but Jem and Fred seem not to notice. Sometimes perhaps a human's feeble sense of smell may be to his advantage. But even Bruin and I now notice it less than when we arrived.

July 1st, 1808.

Fred has been as good as his word, and we now have no fewer than six young bears in our stable, four boys and two girls. All are comfortable on straw beds under a roof that we repaired with slates from a derelict outhouse. Jem required a deposit of £5 per head from their owners to set against the fee for the dancing course of £1 a week, not an unreasonable amount considering my reputation as a former prima ballerina of the bear world. So for the time being we have all the resources we require. However, expenses come rather high with eight bears and two humans to feed, and we are running up quite a bill with a knacker in Kensington.

With the aid of Bruin I am teaching them the gavotte, not a difficult dance. Jem provides the music on his flute, and when he is not there Fred can saw a passable tune on a fiddle.

July 10th, 1808.

On the sunny summer days we have taken to practising our dances in Hyde Park, a short step from our premises. To reach it we walk along

Kensington Gore, skirting the south edge of the private gardens of Kensington Palace. These are open to the public on Sundays, but only to well dressed persons of quality, which we are certainly not. Our dancing floor is a pleasant grove just under the 'ha-ha', a ditch and wall that keep common folk such as us from entering the gardens – though I and any of the bears could scale the wall in a trice.

While we were working our way through a minuet we heard voices from the other side of the obstacle. Looking over, I saw a fat, florid man, considerably overdressed. It was none other than His Royal Highness. He was accompanied by a slim, elegant, immaculately attired man, a thin grey-haired person of slightly shabby appearance, and a fine lady in an elaborate costume. All were applauding our performance.

We bowed deeply – female bears do not curtsey, an act that requires a skirt. At once a mounted equerry cantered up to bid us enter the gardens through a nearby gate, and we were introduced to the royal party. The Prince's companions were Beau Brummell, Muzio Clementi the renowned composer and manufacturer of fine pianofortes, and the Prince's current mistress Isabella Anne Seymour-Conway, Marchioness of Hertford. Understandably, the Marquess was nowhere to be seen; Fred told me later that he is paid to hold his tongue about being thus cuckolded.

The Prince had come to Kensington Palace for a demonstration of one of Signor Clementi's latest instruments, with a view to acquiring one for his own music room – not that he can play a note, but he has people to do that for him. Clementi had caused several pianofortes to be transported down from his house in Kensington Church Street, which was necessary as his warehouse had burnt down a few months ago, causing him a loss of £40,000. Royal patronage will help him to rebuild his fortunes. Also, he has just secured the rights to publish the music of the famous German composer Herr Beethoven, a lucrative contract. So he can weather the near certainty that His Royal Highness will never pay for his instrument.

One of the pianofortes was brought out on to the terrace of the Orangery, where Clementi accompanied Jem's flute to charming effect and we performed several of our dances. Then the Prince, seized by a whim, borrowed some muskets from the royal guards and we bears conducted a military drill with great aplomb until Bruin dropped one of the weapons, causing it to fire. The ball passed through Brummell's elaborately curled coiffure, fortunately not injuring him; but he dropped down in a dead faint to the delighted laughter of the rest of the party. This brought our performance to an end.

We were entertained to a sumptuous cold collation and I consumed several bottles of hock, a delectable beverage which I had never sampled before. The other bears, not to mention Jem and Fred, were also well served and we reeled home to our stable, buoyed up by a promise of royal patronage – though we know all too well that this will never be honoured.

August 30th, 1808.

We now have as fine a troupe of dancing bears as the world has ever seen. But all is not well. The various people who brought in their young bears for training have not been paying their weekly fees, and indeed they are nowhere to be found, as they are all travelling performers constantly on the move. Our expenses are high: eight active and hungry bears will eat their way through a horse in a week, and though the horses we get from the knacker are broken-down, scrawny old creatures they still cost money, and he refuses to extend us any further credit. Add to this the expenses of the two humans and the small rent of the old stable, and we have a precarious financial prospect. Jem is down to his last few silver spoons.

Jem and Fred believe that we should 'up sticks' and go on tour with the troupe, a plan fraught with uncertainty as the six young bears are not legally ours. We are holding them against non-payment of fees, and a bodyguard of united bears would make it hard for the owners to reclaim them, but that is an argument that would not stand up in a court of law.

September 2nd, 1808.

Our minds have been made up for us, but not in the best of ways. One of our neighbours told us that the dreaded Bow Street Runners had been sniffing around our premises, and that he had heard a rumour that they were investigating the theft of some silver from a nobleman.

It would be prudent to leave the country for a while. The resourceful Fred has some friends in Folkestone, who are traders in brandy and other commodities best brought into England without paying the exorbitant excise duties imposed by the wretched government to support their pointless wars. He believes that he can secure us a passage to the continent in return for favours received.

We leave at dawn. I shall miss our comfortable stable and the pleasant routine of dance practice, but all good things must come to an end.

September 10th, 1808.

We have arrived in Folkestone. During our journey we gave several performances on village greens and in the yards of coaching inns, and I am glad to say that we have proved that we can make enough money to support ourselves. On our last night in Ashford, our collection took up £13 4s 2d, the most we have ever earned.

But the law will pursue us, and we need to find a ship. The local advice is that it would be foolhardy to travel to France or Spain, though smugglers' vessels would readily carry us to either, and that the best choice is Portugal. A British force has recently landed here under the command of Lieutenant-General Sir Arthur Wellesley, a rising young officer who has already secured some early success in this campaign.

September 12th, 1808.

We are at sea, in a perfectly legitimate English merchant vessel, the *Buzzard*, bound for Lisbon loaded with gunpowder and cannonballs. Despite the vital importance of the cargo, most of her crew had just been seized by the press gang, and the master, one Roger Boyes, was happy to take all of us, bears and men, as able seamen for the voyage. We bears can climb the rigging with the best of them, and I have been teaching the cubs how to tie a reef knot and a bowline.

We have also been practising the hornpipe, to the delight of the sailors. The diet of salt beef boiled to rags in sea water and accompanied by weevily ship's biscuit is disgusting, but we only have to endure it for a few days. Jem points out that in a war there are always plenty of dead horses, and we are looking forward to them.

I am glad to be on the move again, though it may be to a Europe in the last stages of disorder. There was an incident on our last night in Folkestone which put me in mind of an earlier dissolution. Fred had been out carousing, and returned to his room half seas over with a hussy on his arm. Shortly afterwards we heard derisive female jeers. Fred is not in his first youth, and it seems that – how shall I put it? – his elderly member had failed to rise to the occasion. I remembered my days in the Trinity College library where I read a poem by Maximianus, the last Roman poet, who wrote in the sixth century as the western empire tottered to its end and the barbarians were already within the gates. He had enticed a pretty Greek girl into his bed, but found himself in the same unfortunate predicament. She burst into tears, and when he asked her why, she replied, '*Nescis. / Non fleo privatum, sed generale chaos*', 'You do not understand. I weep not for your collapse, but for the collapse of everything.'

4.

We are in port at last, and I am glad to have my paws on the ground.
It was a difficult passage out of the Channel, and we had to tack every
few minutes till even the strong young bears were almost prostrate with
exhaustion from handling the sails, but as soon as we passed Ushant and
were able to turn south we made good headway. Even the notorious Bay
of Biscay smiled on us, though I have known some gales there when all
on board thought we were lost.

Lisbon is a fine city with many new buildings, having been almost
entirely rebuilt after the calamitous earthquake of 53 years ago. But our
motley band can find no home in the spacious streets created by the
decrees of the Marqués de Pombal, and we are lodged in a smoky inn
on the outskirts.

The day has not been without incident. No sooner had we settled in
our rooms than we heard the roaring of a bear in pain in the street and,
looking from the windows, saw her being sadly beaten with an iron bar
by a villainous gypsy far gone in drink. Naturally we rushed to her aid,
and when the miserable ruffian saw eight angry bears advancing on him,
he fled precipitately.

The poor bear, bruised and bleeding, had fetters around her hind
legs, and our first task was to carry her to a blacksmith to have them
struck off. Fred has a few words of Spanish, and we are able to explain
our needs after a fashion and be understood, but the Portuguese

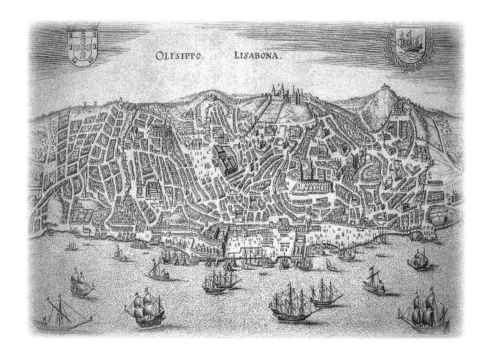

accent is so peculiar that we cannot understand a word that is said to us.

So now we are nine bears and two humans. She is called Angelina, and she is pathetically grateful to us for her rescue. She has promised to teach us some Portuguese dances, which will be of advantage to us in our travels.

It is strange how humans differ when they are drunk. Fred and Jem become jovial and expansive, as we bears do, but in some people strong drink releases a devil inside them. In the wise words of Alcaeus, Οἶνος γὰρ ἀνθρώπῳ δίοπτρον, 'For wine is a peephole into a person.' (I cannot forbear to mention that he wrote in Aeolic dialect, and in standard Greek the genitive would be ἀνθρώπου.)

September 20th, 1808.

Although the invading army of the Corsican tyrant has been banished from Lisbon, the mood in the city remains uncertain. Not long before we arrived, Sir Arthur Wellesley defeated the French general Junot at Vimeiro.

Sadly, his gains have been undone by rascally politicians. Wellesley has been recalled, and the timid Sir Hew Dalrymple has negotiated (if that is the word, perhaps 'surrendered' would be more apt) the Convention of Cintra, under which Junot's forces have been allowed to leave unmolested, under the aegis of the Royal Navy and bearing all their loot, to attack us another day. No one here, Portuguese or English, can see any sense in his behaviour, but I fear it is the way of our politicians to snatch defeat from the jaws of victory. The decision to abandon our attack was taken by Sir Harry Burrard. His men call him 'Betty' – need I say more? But I am sure that the able Wellesley will return to pursue his campaign.

October 1st, 1808.

Angelina has been teaching us the Portuguese dance known as the *vira*, which means 'turn'. It is a lively affair requiring at last eight dancers, four male and four female, circling with front paws raised and sometimes linking with our partners and revolving together. Since we have an unequal balance of the sexes, dear Bruin has gallantly volunteered to perform as a girl, though he grumbles about the humiliation of having to twirl in a skirt. The male bears wear hats, which is apparently *de rigueur* in these parts. These do not fit a bear's head and have to be secured by ribbons to keep them from falling off.

October 2nd, 1808.

None of us is accustomed to the strength of the local wines and our performances tend to be disorderly affairs. Last night we were dancing in an inn, and when we reached the point in the *vira* where the bears link paws and spin in pairs, one of them lost his grip on his partner and both departed in opposite directions into the audience. A table was overturned and a few people bruised, but the incident ended in laughter.

The people have been sadly crushed by the French invasion and we are taking almost no money, but the poorest folk are often the most generous and we are scraping a living, with the aid of rabbits and berries and wild honey and whatever we can gather. It is a far cry from performing for His Royal Highness The Prince of Wales, but we are content and I for one am glad to be on the road again after our sojourn in the stinking fields of Kensington.

October 17th, 1808.

Sadly, the French have returned in force and the war has restarted in earnest. But the news is not all bad. Spanish forces stranded from an earlier campaign in Denmark have been rescue by the Royal Navy, and have arrived in Santander on the northern coast of Spain. British reinforcements under Sir David Baird arrived in Corunna – or, as the Spanish call it, La Coruña – a few days ago. The new British commander, General Sir John Moore, is marching north to meet them, and we shall go with him.

November 20th, 1808.

Fred has procured not one, but two of that wonderful new weapon the Baker rifle – I do not know how he came by them, and indeed would rather not know. Both he and Jem have been skilled poachers when necessity forced such an occupation on them, and they are delighted with the rifle's accuracy. They can bring down a running rabbit at 200 yards, a feat out of the question with the muskets issued to the ordinary soldiers here. The rifle is rather slow to reload, as the ball has to be wrapped in greased leather and rammed down the barrel with considerable force. One would not wish to use it in a close infantry action, but for a sharpshooter in cover it is invaluable.

This evening at the inn where we were dancing, Jem spent several hours beside the fire with a pan of melted lead and some bullet moulds, casting balls for the rifles. I am no warrior, but I wish that the paws of bears were fitted to use such fine weapons.

However, Fred had also found us some cavalry sabres with basket hilts which we are able to grip effectively and with which, I am proud to say, we now exhibit some skill. We have been using the method recommended by Vegetius of practising our strokes by attacking wooden posts fixed in the ground. The posts did not last long when assailed by our powerful paws. Jem made a joke about citizens having a right to arm bears, a reference to the constitution of the new United States which no one else understood except myself, and we exchanged knowing glances while the others looked puzzled.

December 22ⁿᵈ, 1808.

We have been in a cavalry action – not, of course, mounted ourselves, but we are fleet of foot and can keep up with the horses except when they are charging at a full gallop. Yesterday at Sahagún a force of British Hussars under Lieutenant-General Henry, Lord Paget overwhelmed the French cavalry. Our enemy are no mean opponents but, as the battle hung in the balance, we rushed at them from one side brandishing our sabres

and roaring terribly. This frightened the French horses so much that they all bolted. Our men pressed home their advantage and the enemy were completely routed.

Paget himself came to congratulate us, and said that we bears were worth a whole regiment to him. Our bosoms swelled with pride. I confess that I am acquiring a taste for war.

December 31ˢᵗ, 1808.

Bad news: the Spanish under the Marqués de la Romana were defeated by Soult yesterday at Mansilla. Our own men and bears remain undefeated, but we are now clearly on the retreat as we march to Corunna. We have managed to hold off the French in actions at Benavente and Cacabelos. At the second of these engagements, Thomas Plunkett of of the 95th Rifles shot the French General Auguste-François-Marie de Colbert-Chabanais dead at a range of almost 600 yards, and with his next shot wounded the general's aide-de-camp, the even more grandly named Victor de Faÿ de Latour-Maubourg, as he tended his fallen superior. Fred and Jem are full of admiration for such marksmanship, which they can only hope to emulate.

January 17ᵗʰ, 1809.

Things are not going well for us. We have staged a fighting retreat to Corunna, but yesterday Sir John Moore was killed in the final battle. We were with the 15th Hussars on a hill outside the town, pelting the French with stones from a ruined house, when he was struck by a French cannonball. We carried him to safety, but he was mortally wounded and there was nothing we could do to save him. He remained conscious for several hours during which he saw the French successfully beaten off. We have just returned from a sad and silent burial party in the night.

The British forces are surrounded but order still prevails, and our ever undefeated Royal Navy is at hand to bring them off. They cannot, however, take civilians or bears, however valuable these were in previous actions, and we are left on the shore.

The Spanish are understandably bitter, and there have been murmurings of betrayal – never mind that it was their own forces that crumbled first under the overwhelming French onslaught. Jem and Fred have done their best to reassure them that we have only staged a tactical retreat, and will return in greater force – as the damned French put it, *reculer pour mieux sauter*, stepping back to make a better leap. Nevertheless, we feel it advisable to creep away quietly and retrace our steps towards Portugal. Fred and Jem are now sunburnt, ragged, ruffianly looking, and fluent in kitchen Spanish and Portuguese, and no longer look like Englishmen – and a bear is a bear, and no one enquires about its nationality. We also retain our weapons, and quantities of powder and other supplies prudently rescued from the evacuation. It will be a hard journey, but we have seen worse.

5.

Our return to Lisbon will not be like our march north. Then we were travelling with an army in good order on broad roads through a populated area near the coast. Now we are fugitives and must avoid the coastal area, which is swarming with French soldiers. A party of bears is a conspicuous thing, and rumours will be rife of our exploits at Sahagún where we routed the French cavalry. So we must turn east and make our way through the foothills of the mountainous interior, keeping to minor roads or, where necessary, no roads at all.

Yet our little band is not unsuited to such a journey. Nine of us are bears, and at home in the mountains. Fred has been on the move all his life. Jem, originally a city dweller, is now hardened to the privations of rough travel in hostile territory. Looking at him now, bearded, filthy, and swathed in a stinking sheepskin coat he has looted from a French corpse, I can hardly believe that less than a year ago he was a respectably attired manservant serving port on a silver salver to a lord at a famous university.

Fred said to me, 'Daisy, me ole gal, we got an 'ard march in front o' us. I knows yer and the bears can do it, an' so can we. But I got one thing wot I needs to say to yer. When we're in a town or a village, we're two men wiv a bunch o' dancin' bears. But when we're in the 'ills, yer in charge 'cos that's yer country and yer knows best what we oughter do.'

I laid my paw on his shoulder to signify that I understood. Dear Fred, he has no false pride about his lofty human status. We will get him and Jem safe to Lisbon. Our situation is precarious but our hearts are high. To think that last year I was reading Xenophon's Anabasis, about a gallant company's desperate march out of danger in a foreign land, and now we are reliving it!

January 21st, 1809.

We ran into trouble yesterday night, only a few miles outside Corunna: a French patrol, with a corporal and four privates. We were travelling with Fred and Jem at the front, and us bears following at a discreet distance. When Fred and Jem were halted they tried to dissemble, passing themselves off as local peasants, but the corporal was not unintelligent and saw through their pretence. The soldiers were reversing their muskets to give them a beating, but we had already advanced silently into the scrubby undergrowth on both sides of the road, and we descended on the Frenchmen and despatched them with a few blows. It had to be done; we can leave no trace of our passing.

We threw the bodies into a nearby ravine, where they may lie for ever. All over France, many thousands of mothers will never know what happened to their sons. But I have my own son with me, hale and hearty, and he shall be guarded as only a mother bear can.

We went through their pitiful haversacks. As far as military supplies went, there was a useful amount of powder and some bullets that will need to be melted down and recast in the proper size. We threw their miserable muskets away after smashing the locks. Other than that, there were a few loaves of bread, some onions, and four bottles of lamentable wine, all of which we shared out on the spot. The mighty emperor does not look after his troops well. The wine helped to assuage the memory of this sad encounter.

Jem insists on carrying all the powder himself. 'That way,' he says, 'if I gets blown up, it'll be just me and yer'll be right.' He has made panniers out of two soldiers' haversacks and webbing that we can carry on our shoulders. We cannot begin to shoot game until we are into open country.

It is a bitterly cold winter and the men are suffering, though of course we bears are well protected by our dense fur. We sleep in a heap with the men in the middle, in a chorus of snores, and they are comfortable enough.

January 24th, 1809.

Yesterday at sunset we halted at a deserted farmhouse. It had been burnt and the roof was half gone, but one room was sheltered enough. As we were settling down for the night we heard voices, speaking Spanish. Jem called softly to them that we were friends, and we went out cautiously to meet them, with loaded and cocked rifles, to face a couple of ancient blunderbusses pointed in our general direction. A few minutes' parley established that they were local farmers driven out by the French, and now formed into a wandering band seeking retaliation. So we had common cause, and weapons were lowered. They were astonished to find that most of our party were bears, but in war anything may be expected.

They numbered a dozen, cold and hungry, and we shared out today's bag of rabbits and partridges, roasted over a fire for the men but we bears have better teeth and can dispense with cooking. They told us that Ferrol had fallen to the French, and a large quantity of British arms had been captured – not news that we wanted to hear. They themselves had nothing but their primitive guns, a few rusty swords and knives of various sorts, and a burning desire for revenge.

For their style of warfare they used a word I had not heard before, *guerrilla*, 'a small war'. This is the 'Fabian strategy' as conducted by that great general Q. Fabius Maximus Verrucosus, known as *Cunctator*, 'the delayer', who harassed Hannibal's invading army by refusing to confront it directly, instead conducting a series of skirmishes to wear the enemy down a little at a time.

January 26ᵗʰ, 1809.

The Spanish *guerrilleros* stand in need of weapons, and we resolved to get them some. Such an enterprise needs careful planning. We decided to ambush a small French party on a deserted road as far as possible from any villages, lest the French should discover the scene of the attack and murder the local people, as is their bloody custom.

In this sparsely populated countryside there was little difficulty in finding a suitable spot, and Fred and Jem set themselves in suitable firing positions overlooking the road. They planned to shoot the officers or sergeants, and as soon as they had both fired we bears and the Spaniards would come out of the scrub beside the road and despatch the remaining men. It was a day of freezing rain, to our advantage as we guessed that the French soldiers would be less than meticulous in keeping their priming dry in a place where, as they supposed, they controlled the country.

The land is awash with French troops, and soon enough a detachment of fifteen men came trudging along the muddy road, led by a sergeant with a corporal at his heels. Two shots sounded and they fell, then we poured out of the bushes and dealt with the others with claws and knives. Not a shot was fired against us, though I heard a few dismal clicks as flints failed to ignite wet powder. I do not like killing men in cold blood, but the blood of our Spanish allies was hot enough, and not a man was left alive. We dragged the bodies to a convenient escarpment and threw them over. They may never be found.

Our booty was more than enough to arm every man of the Spanish band, but I noted with sadness that many of the muskets were captured British ones of the Brown Bess type. Anyway, they are ours now: not a weapon to rival our Bakers, but good enough up to 80 yards. There was powder and ball aplenty, as well as the men's rations. Well satisfied, we returned to the farmhouse and ate the food and drank the wine. We are now fast allies and ready for further action.

February 5ᵗʰ, 1809.

Last night a red glow in the sky alerted our band, and we hurried down the valley towards it. The French had destroyed yet another village, and the survivors were fleeing the conflagration.

To our relief it was not a consequence of our raid, whose evidence we had, as we thought, concealed well enough. It seems that a farmer had hidden some of his grain store from the invaders, and that was enough to provoke the French into barbaric reprisals.

Our band of *guerrilleros* has grown, and now numbers women and children, all bent on bloody revenge.

February 7th, 1809.

And revenge we have had: fire for fire. The villagers told us that the French were using an outlying house as a powder magazine and store for munitions. We needed more weapons for our increased forces, so we resolved to raid it. Our plan was simple. We would descend on the house at two o'clock in the morning, when sentries are least alert, dispose of them, take what we needed, and blow up the rest.

So it was. The effect of nine roaring charging bears and a mob of furious screaming humans cannot be underestimated. Only a few shots were fired before we had possession of the place and had dealt with the garrison. We took as much powder, bullets, muskets, pistols, swords and provisions as we could carry, and what Jem and Fred could load on to a small handcart we had found. There was a small field gun which provoked some discussion about whether we should have it, but it was deemed too cumbersome for our style of war and abandoned. We lit a long fuse to the remainder of the gunpowder and retreated to a safe distance.

A few minutes later the building went up with a thunderous and satisfying detonation. Looking around me in the glow, I could see savage joy on the faces of all present, and felt it in my own heart. I do not think that I am a civilised bear any more.

Angelina has taken a musket ball in the shoulder, but Jem was able to remove it. I brought thyme from the hillside to make a poultice, which as we bears know reduces the risk of infection. The wound is not grave and she can limp along while it heals, as bears do.

February 8ᵗʰ, 1809.

As Marcus Aurelius sagely wrote, Ἡ βιωτικὴ τῇ παλαιστικῇ ὁμοιοτέρα ἤπερ τῇ ὀρχηστικῇ, Life is more like wrestling than dancing. But there is a time and place for dancing, and for an evening we forgot our troubles. There was food and wine and rejoicing, and we all danced the fandango to the music of Jem's flute and a small guitar played by one of our Spanish friends. Henry, our youngest bear, was overindulged and dozed off in a corner, and we had to carry him to our sleeping quarters in the bushes.

February 10ᵗʰ, 1809.

We have taken leave of our Spanish friends, now a resolute and well armed band intent on the destruction of the invaders, and are heading south again. It was a bittersweet farewell, with rejoicing and boasting of our exploits, but we all know that we would rather be conducting our peaceful everyday lives than skulking in a mountain fastness planning raids on a powerful and pitiless invader. Nevertheless we all accept the decrees of fate, and no one repines.

Even here on the edge of the mountains the French present a constant danger. We march with two bears sent ahead as scouts. Already twice today one of them has come galloping back with a warning, and we have had to change our route. It will not be an easy journey.

6.

March 2ⁿᵈ, 1809.

We are back in Portugal at last. It has been a circuitous journey across ridges and valleys, avoiding the French troops on the lower ground, but we have managed it without any serious encounters. Angelina's wound is fully healed and she is marching with the best of us.

The frontier is marked by the river Minho, or Miño as it is spelt on the Spanish side. We crossed it as far to the east, and therefore upstream, as we could, but it is still a substantial and fast flowing river. That presented no problem to us bears, of course: we could swim across a turbulent river twenty times as wide without turning a hair. But it was not only bears who needed to cross. Jem and Fred can both swim, in a slow and clumsy human fashion – I can hardly believe that humans actually have to be taught to perform this simple act, and drown for not knowing it.

However, as a military expedition we have our baggage, including a stock of precious gunpowder which simply cannot be allowed to become wet. The two Baker rifles, delicate weapons, must also be protected. We do not possess oilskin wrappings to keep things dry.

Therefore, when we contemplated the crossing, we had to find a way of keeping these fragile things above the water. Luckily for us (but sadly not for others) we found the ruins of a farmhouse from which we were able to extract enough charred beams to make a raft.

So we crossed, with the raft propelled southwards by strongly swimming bears, and arrived at the farther shore a few hundred yards

west of our starting point with all our powder dry and, as Fred says, 'everything shipshape and Bristol fashion'. I have been to Bristol, and its fashion is not one I would wish to follow, but let that pass.

On the subject of looking after those rifles, let me mention that we have had difficulty finding a suitable gun oil to keep the bores clean and the locks working smoothly. The only oil commonly available is olive oil, which soon turns to a thick slimy paste and can ruin a weapon in days. We captured a small bottle of spermaceti oil in our raid on the Spanish armoury last month, and Jem has been using it as sparingly as possible, but it will not last much longer.

March 4th, 1809.

Crossing the frontier has hardly brought our band into a place of greater safety. Here too Soult's troops scour the land. Queen Maria and the Prince Regent João have fled to Brazil, as has the entire government, leaving their people at the mercy of the French invaders, and it is up to us to look after the folk that these scoundrels swore to protect.

March 12th, 1809.

As we proceed, we have collected a ragged host of Portuguese infantrymen scattered by recent routs. They have been scraping a starving existence in a hard countryside in cruelly cold weather, as indeed we have, but we are better adapted to such conditions. Loyal to their country, they long to take reprisals on the invaders, but they are unarmed, and their training has not prepared them for the warfare of the *guerrilla*.

Fred and Jem have been taking counsel, and have decided that we must risk another raid on an armoury. We had the devil's luck in our earlier attempt – can we pull it off again? We hear that there is a suitable place only a few miles away, in a commandeered farmhouse a good distance from any town or village. Although we cannot take our unarmed and disorganised Portuguese allies into such an action, we can use them as spies, and so devise the best plan of attack.

March 14ᵗʰ, 1809.

I am writing this with a happy heart – but not with unmixed happiness, as dear Jem has taken a pistol ball in the calf. Fortunately the ball passed through, and we seem to have evaded infection with one of my thyme poultices; but for the moment he cannot walk, and my son Bruin, the noblest of bears, has laid aside his dignity and is willingly playing the role of a horse to carry him about. Jem is stoical and laughs at his misfortune: he would make a good bear.

But to return to the story, we attacked the armoury, as before in the small hours of the morning when we expected the guards to be least alert. A silent charge of bears instantly overwhelmed the outside sentries, and we were into the building in moments. A few men inside were still awake, though drunk, and it was when we were dealing with them that Jem was wounded by a chance unaimed shot. However, we despatched the lot of them, and assessed our booty.

The greatest treasure was six German Jäger rifles, fine weapons though cumbrously long in the barrel. We found a store of balls for them ready cast, with moulds to make more, so if we can train our new allies in their use we have the germ of a little Rifle Brigade.

Aside from that there were muskets, pistols, balls and powder aplenty, as well as swords, daggers and supplies of food and wine. There was even a store of boots, of which our ragged allies stand in sore need. We called them in from where they had been waiting in the bushes and dragged our spoils away, then as before demolished the building with the remaining gunpowder. We earnestly hope that by leaving no survivors, and no trace of our presence, we can as far as possible avoid French reprisals on civilians, the dreadful price of *guerrilla* operations. But in this we can never been certain, as the grim history of the war in Spain shows all too clearly. A raid on a town may seem successful at the time, but too often it proves to be what Herodotus called καδμεία νίκη, a Cadmean victory, in which the conquerors suffer more than the conquered.

March 20th, 1809.

We have now begun the task of forming our motley collection of Portuguese irregulars into a corps of sharpshooters. Trained as line infantry, they know nothing whatever of such skills, and it has to be admitted that we know only a little more; but what we do know comes from our time with the Spanish *guerrilleros*, and they are folk to be reckoned with.

Our first task was to retire to a secluded valley where shots would not be heard, and to find which of the men were the best marksmen; we would award our captured rifles to these. It is not easy to hit a target with a musket, a most inaccurate weapon and almost useless beyond the distance to which one could throw a stone, but by dint of repeated firing were were able to single out those who achieved the most consistent results. We had, and still have, plenty of powder and can afford to be thorough in our trials.

We then had to instruct our chosen men in the art of loading a rifle, a harder task than for a simple musket. The charge has to be measured with greater care, and ramming the ball down the barrel, wrapped in thin greased parchment for a better fit, takes time and strength and sometimes the use of a mallet to force the ramrod in. To achieve two shots in a minute requires considerable training. But, in the words of Epicharmus, τῶν πόνων πωλοῦσιν ἡμῖν πάντα τἀγαθὶ θεοί, the gods sell us good things for hard work.

March 30ᵗʰ, 1809.

We hear encouraging news from the north: the Spanish have rallied and defeated the French at Vigo. Let us hope that the tide is turning in our favour.

Meanwhile, we now have the beginnings of a fighting force. Our men are showing promise as irregulars, as they probably never did as regular troops. They are peasants who know their own territory, and can move across it with ease and freedom. They needed some training in the art of finding a good firing position, not to mention in not shooting each other by mistake, as has nearly happened a couple of times, especially as we are obliged to place all those armed with muskets at the front of any advance, since their weapons are useless at a distance.

April 5ᵗʰ, 1809.

Ill tidings: at Porto to the west, Portuguese resistance has collapsed and Soult now commands this vital port, where he has captured a vast amount of ammunition and supplies. Our men are angry and thirsting for revenge, but what can a couple of dozen men, even with the aid of nine mighty bears, accomplish against the might of the French army?

It would be safer to continue our training and avoid contact with the enemy, but we must let the men put their new skills to the test. With the country again in chaos, we can allow ourselves a direct confrontation with less risk of reprisals against the civilian population. So we are planning another raid on a French detachment, which if successful will both replenish our supplies and keep up the spirits of our little force. Ἐλπὶς γὰρ ἡ βόσκουσα τοὺς πολλοὺς βροτῶν, It is hope that maintains most of mankind, as Euripides wrote.

April 7th, 1809.

Our raid has been successful, but not without cost. Manuel, one of our musketmen, is dead, and two others have slight wounds. Bruin had his scalp grazed by a bullet. As scalp wounds do, it bled profusely, and my mother's heart was wrung as I saw his dear face streaming with blood. But he will be as right as rain in a couple of days.

We waited by a roadside for a French party of manageable size to pass, and at dusk saw a force of about forty artillerymen, with mules dragging five field guns and their limbers. Accurate fire from the rocky hillside sent the mules into panic and they bolted, soon overturning the gun carriages and limbers on the rocky road. Taking advantage of surprise we fell on the men, and there was a brisk exchange of fire followed by a frantic pause to reload, during which we bears accounted for many of the French, and the Portuguese despatched others with swords and daggers. In the next burst of fire our riflemen could do nothing, as foe and friend were mixed together. Driven by fury, we prevailed.

We mourn our loss. But as for the French, our band threw them all over a cliff and, in the words of the Iliad, αὐτοὺς δὲ ἑλώρια τεῦχε κύνεσσιν / οἰωνοῖσί τε πᾶσι, made them spoils for dogs and every bird. However, I must stop quoting the classics, however splendid the poetry. We are not at a little siege of a town in Asia Minor; we confront a tyrant whose intention is to swallow up the whole of Europe into his monstrous empire.

One of the mules had a broken leg. We killed it for a stringy dinner. The remainder we freed: they were probably stolen from the local people, who may find them again. Our supplies are replenished and, thanks to the artillerymen, we have as much powder as we can carry. We intend to continue our journey south to Lisbon. With the northern port in French hands, the returning British forces will be obliged to land there.

Before we left, we buried poor Manuel. One of the men has a little education and was able to mumble a few Latin words of the burial service over his grave. We left it with a sad little wooden cross which wind and rain will bring down in a year. Such are the fortunes of war.

May 2ⁿᵈ, 1809.

At last the British have returned to Portugal. On our journey south one of our bear scouts reported a force in unfamiliar uniforms marching towards us. Jem went out with him and returned in high spirits, shouting 'It's the Redcoats!' I should explain that this colour 'red' is something that we bears do not experience. We can see yellow, green, blue and violet well enough, and can tell the green jacket of an English rifleman from the blue French uniform, but with the red of British forces we are at a disadvantage.

After some discussion, we decided that Fred and Jem should smarten themselves up as far as is possible when one has spent months living in the open, leave their weapons behind, and report to the British officer in charge of the detachment. Wherever they are going, they are our allies and we are in a position to help them, if only in small way.

May 3ʳᵈ, 1809.

Excellent news: Sir Arthur Wellesley has returned and is marching north to confront Soult – and we are of the party. Fred and Jem duly presented themselves. Despite their villainous appearance, all they had to do was to utter a few swearwords to prove themselves English, and they were ushered into the presence of the general himself, where they told their story.

Wellesley had heard of our prowess at Sahagún, of course. It was the talk of every officer's mess for weeks, a battle saved by bears. He laughed delightedly, but not scornfully, at our little offer of help, and sent Jem to bring us for his inspection. We lined up in front of him, twenty-five shaggy bandits and nine shaggier bears, and saluted as smartly as we were able. Wellesley contemplated us with an elegantly raised eyebrow. 'I don't know if they'll frighten the enemy,' he said, 'but by God they frighten me.'

We must be on our way soon. It is three hundred miles to Lisbon as the crow flies, but we are not crows and must thread our way around the hills and valleys.

7.

May 6th, 1809.

We are part of a regular army again, pressing on to confront the French. I must confess that my old bones are aching from the furious pace of our advance. Jem is still limping from his injury, but we found a place for him on the tail of a quartermaster's cart, where he is sometimes joined by Henry, our youngest bear, still only a cub and not equal to the task of keeping up a brisk trot all day.

Wellesley's force is a patchwork affair including two hastily formed Battalions of Detachments, made up from scraps of various regiments disorganised by the evacuation from Corunna. But they have come together into a formidable force and Wellesley, a natural leader to whom his men are devoted, will deploy them with all the considerable skill at his disposal.

Our accidental choice of this cart has proved most fortunate. It seems that the arms include a stock of Jäger rifles captured from the French in some earlier encounter. The British riflemen have their Bakers, so our Portuguese irregulars, most of whom are armed only with muskets, can have their pick of them.

At a brief halt – too brief for this bear! – we inspected the store and the men chose their weapons. Some of them are hunting rifles, shorter in the barrel for easy carrying but still accurate enough. Little João, barely four and a half feet tall, took one of these, a beautiful thing with a carved walnut stock bearing a silver plate with a coat of arms that includes a double-headed eagle. Who knows what deceased German nobleman yielded his weapon to the French invader? But now it is again pointing in the right direction.

Yesterday evening Jem and Fred, aided by those who already possessed rifles, drilled the new owners in the intricate procedure for loading them. It is easy to forget to slide in the safety catch at the rear of the lock when it is at half-cock and you are putting powder in the priming pan, and there was one accidental discharge in which fortunately no one was hurt; at least it reminded them to be more careful. Flints are a constant problem, striking fine sparks until you actually need one, at which point they inexplicably stop working. Fortunately we have a few spare flints already shaped for use.

May 9th, 1809.

We are encamped near the village of Grijó, and our scouts tell us that the French are just over the hill. Wellesley conferred with his officers, and by the courtesy of war that includes Fred, as leader of the Portuguese sharpshooters, and myself, as leader of the bear force. Fred is to take to the hills and harry any French advance; we are to stand ready to panic the horses in any cavalry charge. We were delighted to see Paget again, beside whom we had routed the French at Sahagún. And Wellesley, who has only 35 riflemen from the famous 95th Foot, is pleased to have a further 25 Portuguese riflemen, their sharpshooting skills polished by collecting game for the pot on our travels.

May 10th, 1809.

So far the engagement has been inconclusive. The splendidly dressed Major General Stapleton Cotton, known to his men as 'Lion d'Or', displayed his golden frogs to the Froggies and they hastily fell back upon the village. We have not been in action.

May 11th, 1809.

Battle was joined in earnest today. We bears were with Paget's cavalry, ready to repel any French cavalry. The English horses are used to us, many of them remembering us from Sahagún, and we have been

accustoming the others to bears by ambling peaceably among the lines. We met the French in the early afternoon, and our charge from the wooded sides of the valley had its effect. But it was a stiff engagement and there are many casualties among the men – though I am selfishly glad to say that the bears received only a few scratches. In the heat of action guns are aimed at people: they forget us.

Later, Wellesley sent the King's German Legion to attack the French on one flank and the 16th Portuguese to take on the other, while he advanced on the village of Grijó. The French withdrew to the wooded hillsides, and it was the devil's own task for our motley collection of riflemen to take them out one at at time. But by nightfall we had dealt with them well enough, and the survivors withdrew.

Our Portuguese irregulars, thankfully unscathed, were ecstatic at their success, and bears and men danced around together to the music of Jem's flute. They have lost what little they had in this bitter war, and any advance is cause enough to rejoice. As Seneca says,

Minus in parvis Fortuna furit,
Leviusque ferit leviora Deus.

Fortune is less harsh on the humble,
And God strikes the weak more lightly.

May. 12th, 1809.

Fred said to me, 'That Wellesley cove, 'e don't 'ang abaht.' Never were words more truly spoken. Fresh from our victory at Grijó, the General pressed directly onward to Porto.

At once we met a serious obstacle: the Douro river, wide here where it is about to discharge into the sea. In falling back on Porto, Soult had of course taken the boats to the north side, so there was no way for our men to cross. We found just three which they had missed, not enough to transport our force in good time.

Bears came to the rescue again. Rummaging around the quays on our side, the men found enough rope to span the river, and under cover of darkness we swam across with the end and tied it to a barge, which we

quietly unmoored so that it could be hauled back across the water. Our lessons in knots on the ship that took us to Lisbon have served us well. We captured half a dozen barges in this way while the sentries dozed, lulled into incaution by being on the far side of the river.

May 13ᵗʰ, 1809.

Porto is ours, after a brief but furious action. As soon as our forces began to arrive on the north side of the river and take on the French, intrepid Portuguese civilians came to our aid, launching every boat at their disposal to ferry the rest of the men across.

Wellesley captured a seminary on the north bank and used it as a base, to the confusion of the young clerics living there, whom Jem sent to the cellar with a shout of '*Todos vocês, fiquem lá embaixo e mantenham a cabeça baixa*', 'You lot, stay down there and keep your head down' – which may not be good Portuguese but had the desired effect.

The action was mostly hand-to-hand fighting in the streets in which bears armed with cutlasses played a not inglorious part. But the French still had some artillery, and it was trained on our temporary headquarters.

And here there occurred one of those turns of Fate on which wars hang. Standing next to Wellesley and looking over the town, I saw a cannon surrounded by French troops and pointed straight in our direction. Fred and Jem and his men were off in the town, and there was no way of taking out the gun crew. There was a puff of smoke. Usually, when a cannonball is fired, it goes too quickly to be seen, but when it is coming straight towards you it is perfectly visible. The rising ball began to descend, and it was clear that we were in its path. I flung myself on Wellesley and bore him to the floor as the sound of the shot reached us, followed an instant later by the ball, which entered the open window and smashed a hole in the wall directly behind where we had been.

Wellesley had just the time to shout 'Damned bear …!' before he saw what had happened, and then he embraced me with a cry of 'Daisy, my dear, by God you've done it again!' We were both covered with plaster dust and, as I discovered later, I was bleeding from many small wounds caused by stone chips from the wall.

I believe that Wellesley is protected by a vigilant guardian angel, or maybe a devil, which at this moment acted through me, and that he will pass through this war unscathed and victorious, and live to a great age loaded with deserved honours.

May 14th, 1809.

In the aftermath of a victory joy is mixed with sorrow. The bears attended the burial of the dead, and accompanied Wellesley as he visited the wounded. We raised their spirits, as they consider us bringers of good fortune.

There was a dinner for the officers, and Jem, Fred and myself, as leaders of our motley band, were graciously considered as such. Fred, though he has spent his life on the road, is one of nature's gentlemen and can behave appropriately at such occasions, and Jem has learnt the ropes in his life as a manservant. As for myself, I can hold a knife and fork and eat slices of roast mule with the best of them, though to my mind it is tastier served raw and on the bone, and tackled with tooth and claw.

The quartermaster had found a few dozen bottles of port in a fortuitously unlooted corner of the aptly named Warre's port factory – the term used for a warehouse of this noble beverage which is Portugal's principal and best loved export to England. The rest of their year's stock, 3000 pipes of port, had not survived the first visit of our army and later looting by the French. We toasted our victory and drank the health of our gallant allies.

Wellesley asked Fred how it was that he was in command of a company of bears. So Fred and Jem, their tongues loosened by copious draughts, alternately told the story of how we came to be in Portugal. At the mention of Lord Byron, Wellesley's lip curled: 'That scribbling scoundrel,' he said. And when Jem confessed that, not having been paid for more than a year, he had taken his payment in kind from Byron's silverware, the company applauded. Soldiers understand the unspoken rules of war.

Inevitably, the subject came up of how I was able to get Byron his degree. 'Do you mean to say,' asked Wellesley, 'that this bear understands Latin and Greek well enough to satisfy the examiners of a famous university?' I was embarrassed, because this is an accomplishment best kept concealed from public view – but we were among brother officers, and there is a time for the truth. I motioned to Fred, who passed me the school slate and chalk that we use when I have something to tell him.

But what to write, for a band of humans who have been to the best schools, but probably retain, as Ben Jonson said of Shakespeare, 'small Latin and less Greek'? There are three passages that anyone who has studied ancient Greek for more than a moment will recognise: the first few lines of the Iliad and the Odyssey, and the first few verses of St John's Gospel.

The Iliad I discounted: the sad tale of a vain hero who, in a fit of pique over a girl, sulks in his tent and brings disaster on his army. St John's elegant words seemed a little too theological for a company of soldiers in their cups. So it was the Odyssey, and with not a little sentiment of our own situation I wrote:

Ἄνδρα μοι ἔννεπε, μοῦσα, πολύτροπον, ὃς μάλα πολλὰ
πλάγχθη, ἐπεὶ Τροίης ἱερὸν πτολίεθρον ἔπερσεν·
πολλῶν δ' ἀνθρώπων ἴδεν ἄστεα καὶ νόον ἔγνω,
πολλὰ δ' ὅ γ' ἐν πόντῳ πάθεν ἄλγεα ὃν κατὰ θυμόν,
ἀρνύμενος ἥν τε ψυχὴν καὶ νόστον ἑταίρων.

Tell me, Muse, the tale of the versatile man, he who wandered
Widely and long when the sacred city of Troy he had ruined:
Many men's lands he saw and many men's thoughts he discovered,
Many the pains he suffered within his own heart on the ocean,
Seeking to win his own life and gain the return of his comrades.

The men were dumbfounded, though probably half of them could have
managed as much themselves. Wellesley said to Fred, 'So, sir, is it truly
your own shore you seek again?' (He had never called Fred 'sir' before,
but it was now a conversation between equals.)

'Sir,' said Fred, 'we didn't come 'ere to go to war, we was just on the
run. Reckon the war found us, like. But we done all right, to my mind.
We fought our fights, we raised a little band o' *guerrilleros*, an' they done
us proud. But we ain't fightin' men – nor bears – no way. Reckon this is
a proper stand-up war now, an' we ain't got no part in it no longer.'

'It is true,' Wellesley replied. 'You and your bears and your Portuguese
riflemen have served us well, and you have more than earned your
passage home, and you two and the bears shall have it. And a letter
from me to the chief magistrate of the Runners will halt their pursuit
of you. As for the riflemen, I have news. They are to be returned to the
Portuguese army – not to their original regiments, but to a new corps of
sharpshooters, and all of them shall be promoted to corporal and set to
train new recruits. I did not want to tell you this lest you should think
we were poaching them from you, but as things have turned out it is for
the best.'

All cheered, but none louder than Fred, Jem and myself.

$8.$

We are at sea again – on a merchant ship, *Pride of Scunthorpe*, under the command of Jonas Swigger, a jovial captain who was more than happy to take us bears and Fred and Jem as able seamen – or sea bears. We are an asset to any ship.

The voyage has not been without incident. Yesterday we sighted a brig upwind of us, flying the Red Ensign. It closed on us, and we were about to exchange friendly communications when all of a sudden the flag was hauled down and the hideous French tricolour hoisted in its

stead. It was a French privateer, and we had been the victim of a *ruse de guerre* or, as they say in England, a dirty trick, for which we were quite unprepared. Our vessel has a few cannon, as any merchantman must in these troubled times, but they were not run out, and in any case I doubt whether the human sailors would have been able to man them.

The privateer fired a shot across our bows, and open gun ports revealed a row of muzzles pointing ominously at us. We hove to, as we must. But Captain Swigger was not one to yield without a struggle. He conferred briefly with Jem and Fred, who directed us to creep across the deck, shielded from view by the gunwale. As the French closed on us, with the boarding party ready to leap across, nine bears wielding cavalry sabres suddenly reared terrifyingly into view, stopping them in their tracks. A few wild shots from sharpshooters in the rigging of the tossing French vessel failed to strike us, and with one bound we were on the privateer, rapidly reducing the would-be boarders to their component parts.

English sailors followed us with cutlasses and pistols, and between us we dealt with the gun crews. The rest of the French surrendered and threw down their weapons.

The privateer's captain was among the survivors. Trembling, he answered our questions. The brig is called *Incroyable*, and his name is Jean-Marie Couillon, with a licence from the Corsican tyrant to harry shipping and purloin cargoes. It seems that his exploits are all too well known. We threw him into the forecastle with the others and searched the hold.

There was a fair quantity of brandy and tobacco, no doubt stolen from honest traders. We took this on board without delay. Captain Swigger conferred with Jem and Fred who, now the leaders of a successful boarding party, could no longer be considered mere crewmen. They agreed that we had just enough men and bears to take *Incroyable* as a prize and sail her to England. We bears are to be the prize crew, and the men are to do what they can to keep *Pride of Scunthorpe* pointed in roughly the right direction.

May 25th, 1809.

Incroyable is a well built vessel, dry and weatherly, and a delight to sail; but the French have left her in a most slovenly condition. If we are to get a good price for her, she must be shown at her best. We have been scrubbing the woodwork, polishing the brass, and holystoning the deck to remove the bloodstains. We found a small amount of paint in the locker, enough to patch the more weathered parts of the sides.

May 30th, 1809.

We sailed in convoy across the stormy Bay of Biscay, around Ushant, and past the Lizard and Start Point. We cannot let the French sailors out of the forecastle, where they have been subsisting on a scant diet of weevilly ship's biscuit and green water, and have had to man – or rather bear – the vessel unassisted. But she is speedy and tractable often we have had to shorten sail to allow *Pride* to catch up with us.

Our frequent delays in keeping pace with the slower ship have given us much practice in handling the sails. With only eight aboard a two-masted brig we would usually be considered undermanned, but we are bears and can haul many times more strongly than a mere human, and are now working with an alacrity that would be the envy of His Majesty's Navy. It is then the task of little Henry, smaller than the other bears, to stand at the wheel, and I have been training him in this necessary skill. Despite his tender years he is a bear of good sense, and we all trust him completely.

How can I express the delight of being in command of a ship, the wind singing in the rigging as she responds to the turn of the wheel while eager bears stand ready to trim the sails? It is the joy of the dance, but in a different theatre. This time is, in the words of Homer, δόσις δ' ὀλίγη τε, φίλη τε, a rare gift and a precious one.

Fred came across in a boat to tell us what he and the captain had planned. Of course, it is strange for a merchant ship to capture a privateer, but they are confident that the usual rules will apply: the Admiralty will agree to buy her from us, and the prize money will be shared out among our crew.

Not for her full value, I wrote on Fred's slate.

'O' course not,' said Fred. 'But it's a dirty business and yer does what yer can. One thing, though – we ain't givin' 'em that brandy and baccy, no way we is. The captain knows some folk who'll give us a good price for it. So we'll be stoppin' shortly to land 'em.'

So now we add smuggling to our repertoire. As Ovid said, *Video meliora proboque; / Deteriora sequor,* I see better things and approve; I follow the worse.

June 5ᵗʰ, 1809.

Under cover of night we anchored off a small cove on the Dorset coast in which lies the tiny fishing village of Eype, accessible only by one small lane, an ideal spot for clandestine activity. June 4th is the King's birthday – poor mad old monarch! – and we hoped that the excisemen would be celebrating it properly in a Bridport inn.

Captain Swigger, Fred and Jem went ashore in a boat to make the necessary arrangements, and returned in two hours to say that all was well. Bruin, myself and two other bears went across to *Pride* to help with the barrels. We will also be useful in the landing party in case any of the folk on shore decide to renege on their bargain.

We waited for the signal, five flashes from a covered lantern on the cliff, and rowed ashore with muffled oars, to meet a furtive party who had at least had the good sense to bring a mule and a wooden sledge to haul our cargo up the stony beach. There was a chink of money being counted. They had kept their word – which, Captain Swigger remarked, 'is more than we can expect from the bloody Admiralty'.

Away before dawn, bound for Portsmouth.

June 7th, 1809.

We approached Portsmouth knowing that the outline of the notorious *Incroyable* would be all too well known to those on shore, but we hoped that our steadfast display of the Red Ensign would at least secure a delay in which we could explain ourselves – though it was the same flag that had been used to trick us, newly washed and patched with pieces from the red part of the damned tricolour as well as we could, for sewing does not come easily to a bear. The presence of the familiar *Pride of Scunthorpe* following close behind would be reassuring.

We eased in under topsails only. Four bears to each mast to haul the larboard and starboard clewlines and buntlines, and the sails were up in a trice. Almost before the anchor had struck bottom we had raced up the shrouds and were furling the sails trimly on the yards. It was an arrival to be proud of, and we were sure that it was noticed.

Pride arrived more slowly and less elegantly, and the crew bundled up the sails somehow, in the manner of merchantmen. We were not surprised to see a cutter heading out promptly to meet us.

However, the men aboard the cutter were very surprised indeed when, in response to their hail, eight bears' heads appeared over the

gunwale. I think they might have fired on us, had not Fred's reassuring voice sounded through a megaphone from the deck of *Pride*: 'All's well, sir! That brig there's a prize, an' them's English bears, an' fine sailors too. Pray come aboard 'ere an' we'll 'splain it all to yer.'

I though it best to attend the discussion so, when the men had climbed the rope ladder to the deck, I dived into the sea, swam rapidly across, and went up the ladder, arriving dripping on deck to their consternation. ''Ere's Daisy,' said Fred, 'captain o' the prize. Daisy, meet 'is Majesty's Lieutenant Snipe.' I held out a paw and, to his credit, the officer shook it.

'So these are the famous bears,' said Snipe. 'We have heard wild rumours of their doings in Spain. Is it true that they routed the French cavalry?'

'Indeed it is, sir,' replied Fred. 'An' twice too, at Sahagún and Grijó. An' now they gone and taken that there brig. We wouldn't be where we is now wivout 'em, in fack we'd be guests o' Boney.'

Jem added, 'An' we got the crew – them as is left of 'em – shut up in the fo'c'sle of Ink Royble. She ain't damaged a bit, neither. Would yer like to see 'er, sir?'

We went down the side and rowed over to the brig. The bears lined up as we climbed aboard and gave the Lieutenant a smart salute. He looked approvingly at the clean deck, the neatly coiled ropes and shining brasswork. 'A trim little vessel,' he said. 'I reckon she could fetch fifteen hundred at the prize court.'

A few yells of French execration sounded from the forecastle as we passed. 'There's sixteen in there,' said Fred, 'includin' that Cap'n Cullion. The rest was dinner for the sharks after we'd finished wiv 'em.'

'Sadly, I don't think you'll be getting head money for privateersmen,' said Snipe. (He was referring to the traditional payment of £5 for each enemy sailor captured.) 'In fact we've heard some nasty tales about Couillon, and more than likely he'll be facing trial for piracy and an appointment with the hangman.'

The Lieutenant returned to his cutter, promising to return shortly with Marines to take off the prisoners. 'Did you 'ear that?' said Jem. 'Fifteen 'undred quid! Even after it's shared out wiv the *Pride* we'll be rollin'. An' that's on top of what we got for the brandy an' baccy.'

We had netted £500 for our smuggled cargo, shared out with a quarter for the captain and the rest divided among us – twenty-two men and eight bears getting £12 10s each. If *Incroyable* raised the promised sum, each of us would benefit by a further £37 10s. Though we bears are not much moved by the prospect of wealth, we capered around the quarterdeck as Jem played a merry jig on his flute.

Two hours later the cutter returned and the prisoners were herded into it by stony-faced Marines. 'Reckon you'd best come ashore with us, and bring all the bears,' said Snipe. 'We'll put your boats in tow for you to get back. Word's out in the town, and folk would like to see you. I think you'll be pleased with your welcome.'

And so we were. The honest citizens (and, I have no doubt, the dishonest as well) lined the quay as we arrived. We were garlanded with flowers and led in a triumphant procession through streets lined with cheering crowds. I have never been so proud of my gallant band of bears.

We halted in front of the Guildhall, where an impromptu celebration was held. But first, Fred had to make a speech from the steps. Blushing with embarrassment, he delivered a halting and modest account of our adventures in the peninsula, interrupted by frequent cheers.

We were plied with ale, and there was music from a Marine band – but, as Xenophon put it, ἥδιστον ἄκουσμα ἔπαινος , the sweetest sound is praise. We danced with the townsfolk till long after midnight, then reeled back to the quay, carrying little Henry who had been overcome and was snoring. We rowed in a splashy and disorganised manner back to our ships, and collapsed on the deck under the warm summer stars.

9.

June 25th, 1809.

We are returned to London. Our journey from Portsmouth was necessarily a slow one, as no stagecoach driver will countenance adding eight bears to his passengers. In any case, Fred deemed it prudent to conserve our little fortune from the sale of contraband, for our future in uncertain. So we walked the long road, alternately dusty and muddy, spending the nights in barns and subsisting on what Fred and Jem could shoot and we could catch. Once our day's bag included a sheep brought in by Bruin. No questions were asked.

We were not troubled by footpads. One evening there a sound of scuffling in the bushes beside the road, and we saw several men running away. Eight bears sometimes do have that effect on people.

We halted near towns on our route – Petersfield, Hindhead. Guildford, Cobham, Chessington, Mitcham – and found inn yards where we could perform. Fred, the consummate showman, has worked up an act in which we recreate our adventures in the Peninsula through a series of dances, which we perform to the music of Jem's flute while he tells the tale of our battles. By the time we reached the outskirts of London this had grown into a species of ballet which took over an hour to enact in its entirety and, to judge by our reception, was much liked by the audience. We arrived with an additional £64 16s 8½d in our purse. We do not know who gave us that halfpenny, but bless this economically charitable soul anyway.

On our return we visited our old quarters in the malodorous market gardens of Kensington, and discovered that no new tenants had been found, so we rented them again, for less this time after Jem had pointed out to the landlord that his premises had remained empty because 'Nobody'd want to live in a place what stinks of shit.' To be fair, you hardly notice after a day or two.

Fred visited London to enquire at the Admiralty about the progress of our prize claim. Not surprisingly, nothing had happened. He deposited our little fortune with Cox's military agency at Craig's Court in Whitehall, which often sees money from doubtful sources and does not enquire too closely into its provenance. As Vespasian remarked about the receipts from the public lavatories he established in Rome, *pecunia non olet*, money does not stink. Besides, it is a convenient place to receive any rewards that their naval Lordships might be kind enough to grant us.

Fred also took the opportunity to deliver Wellesley's letter exonerating Jem from blame to the chief magistrate of the Runners. We trust that this should be the end of the affair.

Our old stable was not without a tenant. A ragged boy was asleep in a corner beside a cage containing a few bedraggled chaffinches. When he woke to find himself surrounded by bears he was seized with panic, but after he had calmed down he told us in broken English that his name was Giulio, and that he was an Italian orphan who sustained a miserable living by exhibiting his birds in the streets.

Many of us bears have seen the misery of captivity – the chains, the painful nose rings, the heavy sticks. We could not leave those birds imprisoned. We told Giulio that we would look after him as well as we could, but the birds must go free. To this he agreed, and we opened the cage and our hearts were lightened as they flew out.

June 27ᵗʰ, 1809.

The chaffinches did not go far. Accustomed to captivity, they are hopping around our quarters, and a pair has started building a nest in a bush outside the stable door. We constantly hear their simple song, a succession of quick notes accelerating into a trill and turn. Jem can imitate this admirably on his flute but, having perfected it, no longer plays it, as it sends the male birds into a frenzy of emulation.

We have included Giulio and three of his ragged friends in our ballet, playing the part of Portuguese irregulars. They are quick to learn and delighted to have a purpose for the first time in their brief lives.

July 5ᵗʰ, 1809.

We were practising our dances in Hyde Park on Buck Hill, a slight eminence whose northern end overlooks the royal gardens. Whom should we see but His Highness the Prince of Wales, taking his morning exercise on one of the newly fashionable Velocipedes with his paramour the Marchioness of Hertford, and accompanied by the Duke of York?

No sooner had we noticed him than there occurred one of those accidents that sadly often attend the riding of these machines.

But, nothing daunted, the royal party picked themselves up and, having heard the merry music of Jem's flute, recognised us and waved cordially. A hastily dispatched equerry conducted us into the royal precinct through a gate in the bastion, and we took His Highness's mind off his bruises with a spirited rendition of our new performance. He was delighted, and said that we should have a chance to entertain his friends with it.

July 7th, 1809.

While it may be unwise to trust the word of princes, when it is in their interest to respond they do so with alacrity. This morning a messenger delivered a Royal Command in a beautiful cream-coloured envelope bearing a wax seal impressed with the royal coat of arms. We are to attend a ball at Carlton House in six days' time, and perform for the guests. On the previous afternoon we are expected to rehearse our performance with the royal musicians.

All are tingling with anticipation, and our dances are well enough rehearsed, but there is the matter of clothing. Fred and Jem will need to be attired, if not in the dizzy height of fashion, at least well enough to gain admittance to a palace. The four boys will do well enough in their own ragged clothes, for the poor look much the same anywhere.

But what of us bears? After some discussion, we agreed that the males should wear waistcoats of various colours, and the females should have ruffled skirts similar to those we used for our dances in Portugal, though the original garments vanished long ago under the exigences of war.

July 8th, 1809.

One of Giulio's sisters is a seamstress, and has agreed to make us the necessary garments for a reasonable fee. Fred has been to Whitehall to secure the necessary monies from the bank, and we have visited several pawnbrokers' shops to find suitable garments for the men and curtains that can be transformed into costumes for the bears.

July 11th, 1809.

Our finery is ready, and we make a brave show. Perhaps the men's evening dress is a little threadbare and patched at a close inspection, but no one expects us to pass ourselves off as aristocrats, and the effect is good enough from a moderate distance. The bears' clothes, a riot of colour and flounces, are magnificent. Never was there such a fine ursine party.

July 12th, 1809.

We attended Carlton House for the rehearsal. It is a new and extensive building to the west of the King's Mews at Charing Cross, and is appointed in a style of showy magnificence. A wooden stage has been set up at one end of the enormous ballroom, and it is here that we are to perform.

His Royal Highness paid a brief visit to the proceedings. He was looking a trifle jaded, perhaps having indulged himself the previous night a trifle more than is fitting for a person who, at 45, is no longer as resilient as he was in his youth. In the words of the proverb, *Voluptati moeror sequitur*, Sorrow follows pleasure.

I cannot speak very highly of the orchestra. Professional musicians are at best unreliable, and often arrive without having glanced at the music they are to play; then they complain that their part is too difficult. Sometimes they send substitutes to the rehearsals and arrive at the actual performance completely unrehearsed – and sometimes they do the opposite, which is worse.

It made me long to go back a hundred years to the court of King Louis the Fourteenth of France, whose renowned string orchestra, Les vingt-quatre Violons du Roi, played like no musicians before or since – probably under pain of death, but who would miss a few fiddlers?

Anyway, the players scraped their way well enough through the few popular tunes we use in our performance. The English audience are used to such things, and it will do. As Euripides wisely remarked, Δεὶ τοῖσι πολλοῖς τὸν τύραννον ἀνδάνειν, It is necessary for a prince to please the many. But Jem's lively flute is more agreeable to my ears.

July 14th, 1809.

Last night's performance was a triumph, and we are all glowing with pride. Our ballet was the principal act of the evening, as it deserved, and the account of our exploits in the war was received rapturously by the audience, who applauded us for minutes on end as we repeatedly took our bows.

Afterwards, the floor was given to general dancing and we mingled with the guests, whom we surprised with our agility in the latest dances. There was a great deal of food and drink to be had, and we availed ourselves of this as only bears can.

During the performance we had observed that a distinguished-looking man in the audience seemed to be stifling laughter. Fred chanced to meet him as they were waiting to be served at a side table. He was the Italian ambassador, and he told us that the war cries uttered by the four boys playing the role of Portuguese irregulars were in fact foul slanders against the Prince of Wales uttered in the thickest Calabrian dialect, which even he had struggled to understand. The substance of their remarks, as he reported them, makes me blush. Let it suffice to say that certain transactions between His Royal Highness and the Marchioness of Hertford were the principal subject. How fortunate that His Excellency was the only person present who could understand them, and that, being a diplomat, he preserved a discreet silence about what he had heard.

Little Henry had rather too much to eat and drink, and was sick into a silver épergne filled with roses. Luckily this passed unnoticed in the general mêlée.

As we left, I observed that the boys were clanking slightly as they walked. Fred and Jem halted and searched them, and relieved the four of them of what I estimate as eight pounds of silverware, to their disappointment. As you would expect, Jem is now slightly sensitive about such petty larceny, and handed the haul back to the major domo. 'Lord bless you,' was the response. 'But there's no need. You'd never guess how much the nobs snaffle at these affairs. Why, I reckon as how we lose near five hundredweight of silver a year.'

It seems that the Prince of Wales simply orders more from Messrs Mappin & Webb, and that they are the real losers because he has not paid their bills for the past twenty years and more. The price of a Royal Warrant is a high one.

Jem now regrets his honesty, though not as much as the boys do. Still, we have profited by 50 guineas from the evening's entertainment, and (unlike the unfortunate royal cutlers) we were paid on the spot, in gold. The money will be fairly distributed among us, and the lads' share is probably more than they could have raised from their petty larceny.

We have mingled with the highest in the land, and have achieved what is probably a mere moment of fame. As Fred said to me as we settled down on the straw in our none too fragrant quarters, 'Daisy, me dear ole bear, we done all right tonight. But what're we agoin' a do for an encore?'

10.

July 15th, 1809.

After our success at Carlton House it would be tempting to expect offers from impresarios of the leading London theatres eager to stage our performance. But we have been – bears and men alike – too long in this uncertain business to imagine any such thing. Fred has, after some searching, found us a place on the bill at Crint's Theatre, a small and shabby establishment in Percy Street, which runs between Charlotte Street and the Tottenham Court Road. It has been converted by knocking together three rooms in a house hastily erected 120 years ago by If-Christ-Had-Not-Died-for-Thee-Thou-Hadst-Been-Damned Barbon – son of the hellfire preacher Praise-God Barebones, or Barbon – who preferred to be known as Nicholas but his acquaintances called him Damned Barbon. (He had no friends.) Built without foundations, it has subsided badly, and going up the sloping and irregular stairs is an adventure. But I digress.

The proprietor of this establishment, one Jim Crint, does not inspire confidence. As Fred said, 'We need to keep a close eye on this cove.'

Our place in the evening's entertainment falls between a display by some acrobats calling themselves the Ravioli Trio, though they are actually from Bermondsey, and a recital of patriotic songs by a Mrs Minion, a lady of Greek origin disguised in a ginger wig but touchingly loyal to His Majesty (may he recover from his sad affliction). We have shortened our

performance to half an hour, retaining the most exciting elements, and the drummer of the theatre orchestra has been equipped with two large wooden slapsticks to render the sound of gunfire when required.

July 20ᵗʰ, 1809.

Our first week has gone well, and the audience has been generous with applause. We now remain on stage flanking Mrs Minion as she sings 'Hearts of Oak', 'Rule, Britannia' and other favourite ditties, and she admits that her moderately melodious warblings are now much better received than formerly. We expect to be paid on Friday, tomorrow, after the performance. Fred and Jem will be accompanied by all the bears in case Mr Crint should be thinking of defaulting on his obligations.

July 21ˢᵗ, 1809.

Sad to relate, things have not gone as we had hoped: as Homer so wisely remarked, Ἀλλ' οὐ Ζεὺς ἄνδρεσσι νοήματα πάντα τελευτᾷ, But Zeus does not fulfil all the desires of men. The evening's performances began as usual, and we were waiting in the wings for the Raviolis to finish. They are two men and a woman, the brothers Albert and Arthur Yallop and Arthur's wife Georgina, and much of their act consists of throwing Georgina from one man to another.

At the climax, Georgina was expected to perform a triple somersault in the air as she flew across the stage. But she mistimed her flight and struck Albert in the face with her foot, and they both went sprawling down on the boards, knocking over two of the Argand lamps at the front of the stage which provided illumination for the spectacle. In a moment the hem of her gauzy skirt went up in a blaze. Albert ripped it from her and threw it into the orchestra pit, where it ignited a pelmet hanging from the front of the stage. As the orchestra fled, the flames spread up and soon the curtain on one side of the stage was alight.

As you would expect, the audience fled towards the exit at the other end of the hall – only to find that Mr Crint had locked the door to prevent people from sneaking in without payment, and he and his keys were nowhere to be found. In the panic-stricken press, soon people would be trampled to death. But then we heard the voice of Fred, standing on the blazing stage and shouting, 'Make way for the bears! They're comin' to break down the door!'

We surged into the hall and the people parted before us like the Red Sea before Moses. It was the matter of a few moments to kick through the panels of the door and wrench the frame to pieces, and the audience spilled out into the street.

Outside, smoke was billowing from the windows and a crowd had already gathered, to watch the spectacle rather than to help extinguish the blaze. It goes without saying that the economical Mr Crint had not paid for fire insurance, which might have provided an engine in time to save the house.

As we stood there, another voice was heard: 'It was them bears what done it! Them bears started the fire!' It was the voice of the infamous Crint, who must have escaped through the back door. Most of the crowd had no idea what had happened in the building, and in a moment the mood turned ugly. As people started to shout 'There's the bears! Get the bears!' Fred and Jem appeared at our side.

'Time to go,' said Fred. 'Daisy, form a square.' We had seen enough battles to know what to do. The eight bears closed around the two men, and we marched out roaring terribly until we were at the edge of the crowd. There we broke ranks, ran up Upper Rathbone Place, and escaped through a little alley into Newman Street, from where we were able to proceed undisturbed.

The Italian boys had vanished as if they had never been. 'Can't say as 'ow I blames 'em,' said Jem. 'It was turnin' right ugly back there.'

It was a relief to be back in our mephitic stable in Kensington. But Fred summed up the feelings of us all: 'We can't stay 'ere any longer, me dears. No more time 'angin' around royals an' nobs. It's back on the road for us.'

July 23rd, 1809.

We have left London on the Bath Road, with no idea of where we are going and simply because it was the nearest main thoroughfare to our quarters. By common consent we have abandoned our former act and are simply dancing to entertain the audience. A performance in an inn at the peaceful village of Heathrow brought in the disappointing sum of £3 6s 4d, but this hardly matters, as our travels have taught us to live off the land and we need money for little more than to buy powder and lead to make bullets.

In search of better territory we turned off the main road to the south, and at the moment we are encamped in a barn outside the town of Guildford, and have been considering our future course. Fred was impressed by one of the artists at Crint's Theatre, who conducted a mind-reading act under the name of The Great Mentalist, though he was actually called Saul Dunnock.

Mr Dunnock worked with an assistant, his wife Rachel. The stage was divided with a solid and perfectly genuine partition, which sceptical members of the audience could examine on request. They would come on stage and hand any article to Rachel, who would ask her husband, on the other side of the partition, what it was – and he would make his answer to her and the audience, almost always correctly.

The secret, of course, was in the words she used. There are a thousand ways of asking 'What do I have here?' and they had worked out a code to describe all the things that people in the audience would be likely to have in their pockets and bags – coins, pens, knives, combs, books and the like. For example, 'What do I have?' meant a house key, 'What is this?' meant a Bible, and 'What am I holding?' meant a watch. If you added 'here' to any of these it signified that they were large, but 'in my hand' meant that it was only part of an object.

July 25th, 1809.

Fred could remember only a small part of the elaborate code, but that did not matter, as every pair of performers must have their own private language and learn it by constant rehearsal. Of course I am playing the role of the Great Mentalist, and writing the answer with chalk on a board. I am to be Daisy the Discerning Bear, and we hope that the novelty will be well received.

We have been practising in every spare moment, with some success. Meanwhile our gallant band sustains itself by capering about in inn yards, shooting rabbits and wood pigeons, and scrumping early apples from orchards.

July 28th, 1809.

We are now at Farnham in Surrey, and this evening we tried out our new act publicly for the first time at the Queen's Head inn. It went very well, for if you do not know how it is done, the spectacle is genuinely amazing. I successfully named a purse, a lead pencil, a watch case without a watch ('What am I holding in my hand?'), an onion and a fan.

Then I sensed that Jem was in trouble. After a pause, which he disguised by sneezing and blowing his nose, he asked awkwardly, 'Tell me what's this odd thing 'ere what I bin given?' 'Tell me' meant that the thing was not on the usual list of objects. 'Odd' meant 'made of wood', 'here' that it was large, and 'given' that it was long. From that description I could not guess much, so I wrote on the board 'A big long piece of wood, but I know not what it is.'

There was long and loud applause, and Fred held the thing up for me and all to see. I recognised it as a weaver's shuttle, but half the audience would not have had the least idea what it was. Sometimes a near miss can be better than a hit. And, as Periander remarked, Μελέτη τὸ πᾶν, Practice is everything.

Our evening's collection amounted to the goodly sum of £15 7s 1d, as well as a small silver coin depicting the Goddess of Liberty with flowing hair. It was an American 'half dime' – the word comes from *decem*, ten, and a dime is worth ten cents and a half dime five. We shall keep it as a token of good luck.

August 5th, 1809.

It goes without saying that all the other bears, encouraged by my success, are eager to pursue specialities of their own. My dear son Bruin has ambitions to be a fire-eater, and has been practising this art for several days. His fur is now slightly singed in places, but he assures me that he is getting the way of it.

We found an old zither going cheap in a curiosity shop in Farnham, and Angelina is learning to play it. This instrument is very suitable for bears with their rows of strong claws, though we struggle with the violin or the hautboy. She can already manage two Portuguese dances and a passable rendition of 'God Save the King'. She practises assiduously and I am sure that her skills will improve daily.

Jem found a discarded handcart in a rubbish heap, and took its wheels and has used them to make a small Velocipede for little Henry. It is not a difficult device to master, and on a smooth surface he can now ride it while standing on the saddle. There is the germ of an impressive performance here.

William believes that he can learn sword-swallowing, and has been experimenting with an officer's dress sword – that is, a sword with a fine gilded hilt and a length of plain metal in place of a blade – which we found in the same shop. This is not an easy skill to learn, and much retching has been heard on the outskirts of our encampment, but he has been saved from injury by the bluntness of the sword and I am sure that his efforts will eventually be crowned with success.

Mary has been teaching herself to juggle. She can already keep four pine cones in the air.

Emily and Peter have been working on a seesaw performance, though this has had to be set aside for the moment after the builder's plank they were using snapped under their weight. No matter, we shall find another.

Fred has been trying to think of a name for us, but after much cogitation has not been able to do better than 'The Amazing Bears'. And why not? We are boldly going where no bear has gone before. As Ovid said, *Audentes Deus ipse iuvat,* God himself helps those who dare. Who knows what we shall accomplish?

11.

September 5th, 1809.

It has been a busy month. Our aimless wanderings took us to Guildford, where we have been encamped in a tumbledown barn. The farmer is quite content with our presence, as we are usefully reducing the numbers of rabbits, wood pigeons and other pests that would otherwise have despoiled his crops. For our part we are happy to walk down the edges of fields, close gates behind us, and generally behave as responsible people do in the country.

Occasional performances in the inns of Guildford and on village greens bring in enough money for our modest needs, but on most days we practise our skills in a clearing in a nearby wood. Bruin's fire eating is now of a high standard, and he has progressed from the simple skill of extinguishing torches with which every fire eater begins his act, through the more advanced tricks such as transferring a flame from one torch to another on his tongue, and finally to the spectacle that the audience are waiting for, the 'blow out', in which he appears to shoot a long jet of roaring flame from his mouth.

The torches are metal rods with string bound around the tip to absorb a small amount of ordinary lamp oil. There is not much heat in them, and the flame can easily be extinguished by putting the torch in the mouth to cut off its supply of air – though the flame is real enough, and blisters are a constant trial to the performer, who simply learns to ignore them. The 'blow out' is done by taking a small amount of oil in the mouth a blowing it out in a spray past a burning torch which ignites the vapour. Bruin has to be very careful when performing this trick in the yard of an inn with a thatched roof, and we always have several buckets of water on hand – something that would have saved Jim Crint from the loss of his theatre.

Little Henry's Velocipede act has developed in a surprising way. He had become adept at balancing tricks, including riding his machine poised on only the back wheel. However, he was limited by the fact that it can be propelled only by putting a foot to the ground and pushing it forward, which limits the length of any trick to a few seconds.

While watching him practise, the ingenious Jem was struck by an inspiration. The ordinary grindstone used for sharpening knives, sickles and swords is kept in constant motion by turning a crank handle. Jem thought, What if the principle of this handle could be used to turn the wheel of a Velocipede, and thus keep it in uninterrupted motion? He and Fred went off to a blacksmith to get the necessary metalwork done, and the result is a most curious machine. It has a single wheel turning upon an upright wooden fork at the top of which is a padded leather saddle. At each end of the axle is a crank, the two facing in opposite directions so that they can be pushed alternately with the hind feet, through wooden blocks free to rotate on the handles – or I should say 'pedals' – which are shaped so as to be easily gripped by a bear's claws. I have christened this device with the impeccably Latinate name 'Unirota'.

Henry was happily astounded by this unexpected gift, and has learnt to ride the Unirota in a few days. He now goes everywhere balanced on his machine, as if it were his natural form of locomotion. It has a particular advantage in that it leaves the rider's front paws free, and Angelina is now teaching him to juggle.

Peter and Emily have abandoned their notion of a seesaw performance after a third plank broke under their combined weight. Perhaps this art is more suited to lighter creatures such as humans. They are now learning to walk on a slack rope. We found a length of strong hempen rope in a store outside the town's House of Correction, and had no hesitation in appropriating it, for it was destined for the attention of the unfortunate prisoners who would have had to unpick it to make oakum, strands of hemp which are mixed with tar and used to caulk the seams of ships. Now the rope is stretched between two stout trees, and the ground shakes with heavy thuds as one of the bears falls off yet again. But they are undaunted. As Plutarch says, Πᾶν τὸ σκληρὸν χαλεπῶς μάλάττεται, Everything that is hard is softened with effort.

September 10ᵗʰ, 1809.

We have had two pieces of good news. Fred has visited London. For the journey he borrowed one of the farmer's horses in return for the trifling payment of six brace of partridges, and he has just returned and restored the placid grey gelding to its owner.

His friends – he has friends everywhere – told him that Jim Crint's baseless accusation against us bears that we started the fire in his theatre has evaporated, and indeed has Mr Crint himself. It seems that he had insured the theatre against fire, which is only prudent as these places constantly burn down, but that the policy did not cover him against a fire caused by his own negligence. He had indeed been careless in his penny-pinching way, for he ought to have rendered the drapes fireproof by painting them with a solution of alum, and had not troubled to do so. By calling a hue and cry upon us, he had hoped to divert attention from his own failings; but the insurers would have none of his story and refused to pay. Pursued by many creditors, Mr Crint has vanished into the wings, and let us hope that his re-entrance is not in the script.

To our delight Fred told us that he had visited the Admiralty, where he was greeted with the most welcome news one could imagine. The prize court has decided to buy *Incroyable*, the French privateer vessel we captured, for £1750 – that is, £250 more than we had expected. The extra price was decided in view of her usefulness as a small speedy ship of war, something of which their Lordships stand sadly in need, as our shipyards still cannot match the French in the construction of such vessels.

We have stayed too long in the provinces. Our performances are well rehearsed, our company of bears and men unprecedented. It is time to return to London and show off our skills. Our goal is, in the immortal words of Homer, αἰέν ἀριστεύειν καὶ ὑπείροχον ἔμμεναι ἄλλων, always to excel and to be better than others.

September 17th, 1809.

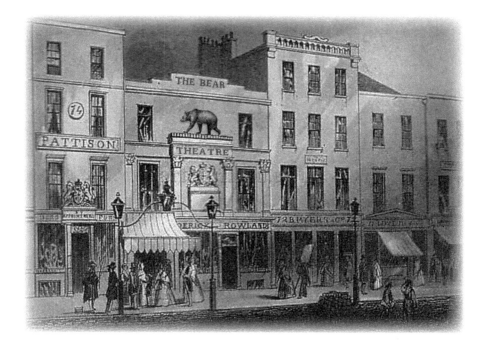

We are returned to London. With our new-found riches, Fred has secured the lease of a theatre in Oxford Street, and we have not delayed in renaming it The Bear Theatre, and have installed a painted plaster statue of a bear on the front. It is spacious but a little decayed and shabby. However, a lick of paint here and there has restored it to an acceptable state. The bears have been helping with a will, and we all smell of the turpentine we had to use to remove the splashes of paint from our fur. Sometimes humans, with their removable clothes, are at an advantage.

We need to live close to the theatre, and Fred has secured us premises in Bell Street, off the Edgware Road and a little way to the north-west of the theatre. The building will soon be demolished to make way for a new row, and it is in a tumbledown condition, but we have seen far worse and it will serve for now.

September 20ᵗʰ, 1809.

There has been much excitement in London. The old opera house at Covent Garden had burnt to the ground a year ago – a common occurrence for all theatres, of course, and how we all wish for a system of lighting that does not involve naked flames! It has been rebuilt, and on the 18th it opened for its first performance, not yet a full opera for which they are not ready, but a staging of Shakespeare's Scottish play, which I will not name for fear of bringing bad luck on ourselves. And indeed, the traditional ill fortune associated with this play has manifested itself.

To defray the great expense of rebuilding and furnishing the new theatre, the management has been obliged to raise the price of admission. They have been quite modest in their demands – for example, a ticket to the pit, which used to cost 3s 6d, now costs 4s. However, the increase incensed the public, especially those who bought the cheapest tickets, and their protests grew into a riot which spilled out into the surrounding streets.

Last night the disturbance continued, and it seems that it will continue for some time. The slogan of the rioters is 'Old Prices', and they carry banners with the letters OP. Performances at the opera house continue with difficulty, but the conflict cannot be sustained and one side or the other must yield.

September 21ˢᵗ, 1809.

'Right,' said Fred, 'we're goin' to 'ave an opera.' He has somehow secured the score of *La Vestale*, a work by the fashionable composer Gaspare Spontini, which created a sensation at its first performance in Paris two years ago. There is a distinct advantage in such a choice: since we are at war with the French, we are at liberty to pilfer their creations without paying them. Thanks to this economy we can stage our performance at 'Old Prices', and we shall have little difficulty in drawing audiences away from the other place.

The libretto is in French, and I am now translating it into English for our performance. That is in itself a novelty, since the opera house at Covent Garden performs its works in Italian, and most of the audience have little idea of what is supposed to be happening on stage.

The plot is risible, as is usual in opera. It is set in ancient Rome, and the heroine is a Vestal virgin, Julia, who is pledged to perpetual virginity and charged with the upkeep of the sacred flame at the temple, which must never be allowed to go out.

Of course – for this is an opera – she is in love with a Roman general named Licinius. Though she strives to shun him and attend to her duties, she is obliged to present him with a wreath when he returns from a successful campaign. The inevitable consequence follows, and while the two are dallying at the temple she forgets to add fuel to the sacred flame, which goes out.

For this grave breach of her duty Julia is sentenced to be buried alive – the Romans were not slack in their administration of punishments. But, by a divine miracle, a thunderstorm relights the flame, and this is taken as a sign that she should be spared – and into the bargain, that she should be released from her vows and allowed to marry Licinius. As it is said, tragedies end with a death, and comedies with a wedding.

September 23rd, 1809.

Fred has engaged a band of musicians and singers, on the strict understanding that they must attend all rehearsals and no substitutions are possible, except in the case of genuine illness.

To play Julia, we have found a young singer named Adelia Catelani, a name to conjure with – though she is not the famous Angelica Catelani who performs to huge acclaim and huger fees in Covent Garden and elsewhere, but her sister-in-law. Nevertheless she sings prettily enough, and we are all delighted with her. In the usual French style, the opera begins and ends with a ballet, and of course it is we bears who will be performing here. They do not have such attractions at Covent Garden.

Fred's plan is to stage our own performance every afternoon, and the opera in the evening. It seems a thoroughly sound idea – and let us hope so, as we have invested all our capital in the lease and repair of the theatre and the hiring of the singers and orchestra. To quote Plautus, *Videte, quaeso, quid potest pecunia*, See, I pray you, what money can do. Let us hope it does what it can.

We are all busy with rehearsals, and eagerly await the first performance on Monday the 25th.

12.

I write this after our customary afternoon performance, as the scenery is being set up for the opening night of *La Vestale*. The past few days have been a furious succession of quarrels and panics, but I suppose that such things are to be expected in the theatre.

The opera itself could not have been better chosen. There are only seven singers, three of them with important roles. These are Julia the Vestal virgin, sung by Signorina Catelani; Licinius the Roman general, sung by a young man with the stage name of Carlo Panini, but who is actually called Charlie Rolls; and Cinna his friend and confidant, sung by Giacomo Savone, real name Joe Soap – how much better things sound in Italian!

We have managed to reduce the orchestra to two violins, a violoncello, a bass, a flute – played by the able Jem – a serpent, a horn and a motley collection of drums and miscellaneous makers of noise presided over by my dear son Bruin, since these are not needed in the ballets that start and end the opera, where all the bears except my old self are on the stage dancing like maenads.

However, Signora Catelani has been, as Fred succinctly put it, a pain in – well, a region that I cannot decorously mention. She insists on her dressing room being larger than those that the other singers have to share: five men are crammed into one room, though they do not complain; and the only other female singer, who plays the role of the Principal Vestal, prepares herself in a little cupboard under the stairs. La Catelani also demands that her room should be filled with roses, replaced daily, and that there should be plates of her favourite liquorice comfits for her voice (which we have had to buy from a ruinously expensive establishment in Bond Street), and Mr Bellamy's veal pies to sustain her already ample girth. Nevertheless, she sings admirably, and we must accede to her demands to keep her twittering. In the words of the ancient proverb, Γυνὴ τὸ συνολὸν ἐστὶ δαπανηρὸν φύσει, Woman is generally extravagant by nature.

She is also involved in a liaison with the horn player, a tall and muscular red-haired Irishman called Sean Murphy, who styles himself Giovanni Patata. We affect not to notice. She has had a violent quarrel with the Principal Vestal, Annabella Panettone – real name Ann Cakebread – and we have had to restrain them from pulling each other's hair out.

La Catelani also objected to having to sing in English, claiming that Italian is the true language of opera. Be that as it may, this work was composed with a French libretto, and I think I have done it a service in rescuing it from that nasal language. I also pointed out that the action

is set in the third century BC, a full thousand years before there was a glimmering of the Italian tongue. But it was my assertion that, if her words could be understood by the audience, she would be all the more applauded, that won her over.

The scenery of the second act – the first act is entirely given over to our ballet – is the temple of Vesta in Rome. The score describes it as *temple de Vesta, de forme circulaire*, but a circular temple is difficult and expensive to reproduce on stage, and we have settled for the customary painted flats. Needless to say, this raised objections from La Catelani, who stridently demanded *un tempio rotondo autentico*. I was able to quash this demand by pointing out that the round 'Temple of Vesta' that survives in Rome is actually the temple of Fortuna Virilis, and that she would surely not want to be accused of participating in a vulgar error. She gave in; I think it was the word 'vulgar' that won this skirmish.

She also insists that her principal aria should be performed a third higher than written, to show off her top notes. I am not enamoured of the screeches she emits at that pitch, but we acceded to her demand. Jem and I had to rewrite all the parts for that number in the new key, a laborious task. The aria is sung as she is about to be walled up in a large black pyramid made of canvas: *Adieu, adieu, mes tendres soeurs, adieu*, which I have translated as 'Farewell, farewell, my sisters dear, farewell', and I must admit that it is highly affecting.

We have taken great pains with the climactic scene where divine lightning strikes the altar and relights the sacred flame. The sound effects are not difficult: Bruin has a thunder sheet – a large sheet of iron which makes a loud boom when shaken – and a big wooden slapstick to mimic the crack of the lightning bolt. But how to make the flash? We consulted that eminent natural philosopher Mr Humphry Davy at the Royal Institution, and he was generous enough to give us a portion of an element newly discovered by himself only two years previously. It is called magnesium and, if a pinch of the powder be set on a dish and a flame touched to it, it will go up in a blinding white flare and scare the audience out of their wits.

Anyway, all this is behind us. The performers are rehearsed, the band is tuning up, and I must be off to supervise the bears' opening ballet. As they say apotropaically in this business, 'Break a leg.'

September 26th, 1809.

The first night was a triumph – I can use no other word. For all her foibles, Adelia Catelani is as fine a singer as ever trod the boards in Covent Garden, or Venice or Milan for that matter. The audience wept when she was about to be immured in the pyramid, gasped at our artificial lightning, and cheered uproariously at the final wedding duet, *Sur cet autel sacré viens recevoir ma foi*, which I translated as 'Upon this altar stone I pledge my troth to thee.' Even the mob in the galleries were in ecstasies, and we had to wait for several minutes before the bears' final ballet in order to clear flowers from the stage. The bears danced with unsurpassed elegance, and when we took our final bows they got almost as long an ovation as La Catelani – though I am grateful that we did not get more, or no doubt she would have thrown another of her tantrums.

Afterwards we all celebrated in the empty seats. Fred had provided two dozen bottles of something that passed for burgundy, and a keg of beer that did not pretend to be anything else, and we were all transported by joy and liquor in equal quantities.

La Catelani and Mr Murphy forgot their pretence and embraced each other. I noticed that her Italian accent was slipping, and increasingly often a London diphthong marred the pure vowels of Tuscany. So did Fred, and after a while he asked her, 'Signora, 'ave yer spent long in London?'

'Lor bless yer,' she replied. 'I 'as to keep up that Eyetalian malarkey for the sake o' me reputation. But I'm jest plain Ellie Dobbs from Bow to me friends. And you all bin good friends to me.'

Fred poured her another glass and said, 'Signora Catelani, we is honoured by yer confidence. But we didn't 'ear that last bit, did we, boys 'n' gals?'

We all cheered and roared in assent, and Fred added, 'An' we'll keep up the roses an' lickerish an' them pies from Mr Bellamy, though I did 'ear as 'ow as it was them pies what done for young Billy Pitt these three years past.' He was alluding to what were alleged to have been the Prime Minister's last words, 'I think I could eat one of Mr Bellamy's veal pies.' But the poor man never took a mouthful, and expired shortly afterwards.

October 2ⁿᵈ, 1809.

Fred reports that we have repaid our investment, and his account at Cox and Kings is again 'back in the black' to the tune of a couple of hundred pounds. But five days of uninterrupted triumph makes one nervous of attracting the envy of the gods. As Pindar put it, Εἰ δὲ θεὸν ἀνήρ τις ἔλπεταί τι λαθέμεν ἔρδων, ἁμαρτάνει, If any man hopes that in doing anything he will escape the notice of a god, he is in error.

And so it was. Our success in drawing crowds away from Covent Garden has made the house's beleaguered manager, John Kemble, sadly envious. The Old Price riots still continue, and Kemble has engaged a prizefighter, Daniel Mendoza, to keep order by breaking heads. At our evening performance, as our fashionable patrons were alighting from

their carriages, we saw an ugly mob bearing cudgels heading up Oxford Street towards us, and none of them uglier than Mendoza at their head armed with a great club three feet in length.

They set upon our would-be audience, and in a moment a scene of genteel diversion became one of bloody conflict. We bears sallied forth, roaring thunderously, and beat Mendoza's men back until they fled, but the damage was done. Several blameless members of the public, who had turned out to enjoy an innocent spectacle, were now lying in the muddy road nursing various injuries.

We took them into a downstairs room and did what we could for them, plying them with brandy and reassurance. One of them, a Mr Silas Armitage, who had travelled all the way from Edgware to see the opera, had been knocked cold by Mendoza's club and had a sad swelling on his bald head. But he rallied, and all of them attended the performance, and we saw him later leaving in his carriage. We heaved a general sigh of relief, thinking that matters could have been worse.

October 4th, 1809.

Indeed worse was to come. There has been no further trouble with Mendoza and his mob, and our performances have continued uninterrupted to universal acclaim. But today, after we had finished the usual afternoon spectacle, a pair of Bow Street Runners presented themselves at the box office, asking for Fred – ominously by his full name, Frederick Rowland, which no one uses.

When Fred appeared he was arrested on the spot, charged with the murder of Mr Armitage, and he was dragged away to the courthouse in Vine Street, where he now languishes.

From what we can discover, Mr Armitage left the performance and returned home in apparently good health, but later that night he complained of an increasing headache. Since he had indeed been struck on the head, no one was greatly concerned – but in the morning he was dead. Blood from his injury had been seeping into his brain all the time, and after a few hours it undid this unfortunate gentleman.

The accusation of murder had been made by John Kemble, who was not present at the affray, but he has a dozen so-called witnesses to the effect that that it was Fred who struck the fatal blow – all of them, of course, members of Mendoza's mob, lying through the gaps in their rotten teeth.

Well, Fred will have his day in court, and we will be there to demolish their story and testify to the truth. On the recommendation of Jem, no stranger to legal proceedings, we have engaged the services of a solicitor, Mr Jeremiah Bundle, who is sure that we have a good case and will secure Fred's acquittal. But, as Charlie Rolls – I beg his pardon, Signor Panini – remarked to me, ''E would say that, wouldn't 'e?'

Despite our uneasiness, performances continue: as the old adage has it, the show must go on. But we are all consumed with anxiety at the absence of dear Fred, our guiding light and inspiration in this uncertain venture. Our make-believe Italians have kept in character by visiting St Etheldreda's Catholic church in Ely Place, where they have lit candles to all saints they could find and prayed with honest fervour for Fred's deliverance. I went with them and, as my candle flickered, I said a silent prayer to St Daniel, the patron saint of prisoners.

13.

October 18th, 1809.

Fred goes up before the judge at the Old Bailey tomorrow, accused of the murder of poor Mr Armitage.

We visit him daily in his cell, bringing bribes for the gaoler and food, drink and news for him. He has been a guest of His Majesty before, though never remanded on so grave a charge, and does not complain. It would be wrong to say that he is confident, for so rotten is the edifice of justice that even the utterly innocent have reason to fear that the roof will fall in and crush them. Yet, as the old adage has it, *Fiat justitia, ruat coelum* – Let justice be done, though the heaven fall.

We have not been idle in his defence, and he has that to comfort him. On the advice of Mr Bundle the solicitor, seconded by Jem who has also had his brushes with the law, we have engaged a barrister by the name of Quintus Heron. Seldom was a man so aptly named. He is tall, grey and skeletally thin, with a sharp beak of a nose and cruel pale eyes. His speech is laconic and rasping, and when he is amused he emits a harsh screech of laughter that would curdle milk. As Jem said, 'I don't like 'im much. But 'e ain't 'ere to be liked, 'e's 'ere to do damage to them bastards, an' I believe 'e will.'

When Jem is not playing his flute in the orchestra he has usually been absent, and has often returned late. During these excursions he has been wearing clothes much more shabby and soiled than his usual attire, and on the following day he has had a long conference with Mr Heron. He will not tell me what the two have been plotting: 'Better yer don't know, Daisy me dear.'

October 19th, 1809.

We closed the theatre for the day of Fred's trial. We could do nothing else, for we were all too racked with nervous strain to perform. Signora Catelani has been in floods of tears, and we are doing our best to comfort her.

What a sad reverse after our triumph! But we cannot protect ourselves against misfortune. In the words of Phocylides, Κοινὰ πάθη πάντων· ὁ βίος τροχός, ἄστατος ὄλβος – Suffering is common to all: life is a wheel, and good fortune unstable.

We arrived *en masse* at the Old Bailey. No one made any protest when nine bears took their seats in the public gallery – we are now part of London life, and even the boys who sweep the crossings salute us as we amble down the streets.

The proceedings opened with the ancient and terrifying call on 'all persons having to do before the lords justices of oyer, terminer and general gaol delivery to draw near and give their attention'. Oh, they had our full attention, and we were as eager as a pack of foxhounds to find

justice. Our judge, Isaiah Gaunt, belied his name – plump, rosy-faced and sleepy-looking. We all prayed that we would stir him to wakefulness.

Fred was brought in between two hulking officers; he looked shrunken and exhausted, and my heart went out to him. For the first time I noticed that he had a few grey hairs. After he had pleaded Not Guilty, we had our first sight of the counsel for the prosecution, one Lucius Pike, a long slimy snaggle-toothed streak of a man who, were it not for his horsehair wig, would look at home in Mendoza's gang. Would our own Mr Heron be able to spike him?

As we expected, Pike's first witness was one of Mendoza's men, who gave his name as Ananias Oates. Under oath – and the Bible must have seared his hand to the bone, though he gave no sign of it – he testified that he had seen the accused strike Mr Armitage on the head with a piece of wood, 'mebbe the leg o' a table'.

It was now time for our champion Quintus Heron to enter the lists and cross-examine the witness. His first question was as sharp as his nose: 'Mr Oates, is it true that you have two previous convictions for perjury?'

Pike, of course, objected that the character of his witness was immaterial and that he was under oath, a vain plea in view of the accusation, and as Heron probed Oates further about his convictions for affray and grievous bodily harm it was clear that he was holed below the waterline and sinking fast. Hope began to grow in all our hearts.

Pike's second witness, one Mucius Slider, was also one of Mendoza's crew. He gave evidence of much the same story – and in almost the same words. I had my eye on the jury, and it was plain from their demeanour that they were thinking much the same as myself.

We all silently cheered as Heron demolished him in the same manner as he had done with Oates. But our fearsome advocate had one further blow to deliver: 'While I would never suggest that you were paid by Mr Kemble to attend this occasion, might I ask you why you happened to be in Oxford Street at this time?' This fine example of apophasis brought Pike spluttering to his feet, and the judge ruled in his favour, but a glance at the jury showed that the shot had struck its mark.

After Heron had dismissed a third witness, Ahaz Mugger, with equal brusqueness, we were beginning to believe that we had the enemy on the run. There was no doubt that the prosecution could call on any

number of ruffians who would perjure themselves for a pittance, but it was equally sure that our advocate had their measure; and no more of them were called.

The next witness was a handsome lady of thirty or so, fashionably dressed and of genteel deportment. She gave her name as Hesperia Fairbrother, widow of the late Sextus Fairbrother of Rankling Hall in the county of Essex, and testified that she had been waiting outside the theatre before attending the performance of *La Vestale*.

'I trust, Madam, that you were not injured in the affray,' insinuated Pike.

'No, Sir, not in the slightest,' she replied. 'But I saw the whole affair unroll before my eyes, from start to finish.' And then she made the now familiar claim that Fred had started an attack on innocent bystanders, and she had seen him strike Mr Armitage on the head with a wooden club.

During her testimony I saw Jem consulting in whispers with Heron and leaving the court rapidly.

It was now time for our man to cross-examine the witness. He began, 'Mrs Fairbrother, I am truly glad to hear that you escaped harm in this unhappy incident. I trust that you were able to attend the performance.'

'I was, Sir,' she replied, 'and was greatly diverted by the spectacle.'

'It is a remarkable entertainment,' said Heron. 'The scene in which Jupiter descends from heaven on a cloud is particularly well contrived.'

'Just so; I was much moved by it,' she said, but was then interrupted by the judge: 'Mr Heron, would you kindly confine yourself to the facts of the case.'

'My apologies, your Honour,' said Heron. 'Mrs Fairbrother, since you viewed the entire incident, would you please tell us what the accused was wearing at the time?'

'He was dressed much as I see him now,' she said, 'in a brown coat.'

'Can you describe his breeches and stockings, madam?'

'I recall that the breeches were black, with white stockings.'

Mr Heron then asked for Fred to be allowed to step out of the dock for a moment, and it was apparent that her description of his nether garments was perfectly accurate. Pike looked pleased – but I knew that he was taking a bait.

There were no more questions. The prosecution rested its case and the court adjourned for luncheon. We passed the time in a coffee-house, uneasily aware that we needed to keep our wits about us.

We returned to see Mr Heron present the case for the defence. His first witness was none other than Mrs Armitage, the widow of the deceased – perhaps it was surprising that the prosecution had not seen fit to call her. She was a trim lady in her forties, dressed in unrelieved black, her comely countenance ravaged by weeping.

After offering his sympathies with a sincerity in which I would have believed had he not been a lawyer, Heron asked her for an account of the evening on which her husband had met his sad end.

Dabbing her eyes with a small lace handkerchief, she explained that she had not been able to attend the performance herself, as she had been looking after her little daughter who had the measles, but that she had urged her husband to go to town without her. 'Alas, would that I had advised him otherwise,' she gasped between sobs. The jurors were visibly affected, and one of them had deployed his own handkerchief.

She recounted that Mr Armitage had returned in his carriage in good spirits, having enjoyed the opera and making light of the wound on his head – 'a bit of trouble with the usual theatre mob' – but that he soon complained of a headache. A glass of restorative brandy had no effect, and he took to his bed, which caused no great disquiet at first, but he was fated never to leave it alive.

'Did Mr Armitage describe his assailant?' Heron asked.

'Indeed he did – a tall heavy-set man in a soiled linen shirt and ragged breeches. After he had struck my husband' – she paused to wipe her eyes – 'one of his companions said to him, "Leave 'im be, Dan, 'e ain't worth yer trouble."'

I was beginning to see a plan unfolding. Pike did not cross-examine her.

Heron thanked her, I think with genuine gratitude, and said that he hoped it would not be necessary to trouble her again.

The next witness was someone I had never seen before, a thin, pale, red-haired girl of no more than twenty, shabbily dressed. She gave her name as Dolores O'Connor.

'Thank you, Miss O'Connor,' said Heron, 'for attending the court at such short notice.' She smiled thinly. I realised that Jem had found her during our recess for luncheon.

Heron asked her where she had been at 6 o'clock on the evening of the murder. She had, she said, been sweeping the courtyard at the back of the opera house.

'Which opera house was that?'

'Why, the one at Covent Garden, o' course. I were workin' there till today, when that Mr Kemble sent me away. 'E said 'e was makin' economies, 'cos 'e was losin' money what with the riots an' that Bear Theatre drawin' away the patrons. But I lost more 'n that, 'cos I ain't got no work no more.'

'On that evening, did you see anyone going through that courtyard?'

'Yes, I seen that Mendoza an' 'is pals goin' out. I thought as 'ow they was off to deal with the Old Price crowd agin.'

'Can you see any of those people in the court now?'

'Yes, I can see that Ananye an' Ayaz an' Mucie sittin' over there', and indicated the prosecution witnesses, who twitched as her finger pointed at them.

'And at the same time did you see anyone coming into the courtyard?'

'Yes, that Mrs Fairbruvver – I can see 'er next to 'em now. She's a – um – lady friend o' Mr Kemble, an' often comes to see 'im of an evenin'.'

'Did Mrs Fairbrother stay long?'

'I didn't see 'er go, an' I was in the yard till nine at least.'

Pike, cross-examining, tried to suggest that she was prejudiced against Kemble because she had lost her employment. Her reply was simply, 'Sir, I'm on oath, an' I'm 'ere to say what I seed, an' no more.'

The next witness was myself, a matter which caused some difficulty. Pike objected that I was not a 'person' within the letter of the law.

Heron replied, 'Sir, we are taught that God has three persons, and only one of them has been a human being.'

To which Pike retorted, 'Are you suggesting that the Lord is a bear?' As laughter resounded through the court, I thought, *I do hope so.*

The judge, intervening, said that he would accept evidence from any creature that could prove itself to be rational. A school blackboard on an easel was brought into the court and set up beside the witness box so that the judge and jury could see it.

I took the chalk and wrote, *Your Honour, I am a rational bear and I am ready to be sworn in.*

Pike objected, 'How can a bear swear an oath? We know that brute beasts have no souls.'

I wrote, *I do not know whether I have a soul. But, like Pascal, I will bet that I have a soul, and I will follow the Lord's commandments that my soul may be saved. If I die and have no soul, I will have lost nothing. But if I have a soul, God willing I will gain Heaven.*

'She cites Pascal! That is enough,' said the judge. 'Daisy, you may lay your paw on the Bible and then write the oath on the board.'

I swear to Almighty God that I shall tell the truth, the whole truth, and nothing but the truth.

Heron then asked me to recount what I had seen. Wiping the board clean to make space, I wrote that before the play I had been outside the theatre, making sure that the people waiting for tickets were lined up in an orderly manner. I had seen a mob coming along Oxford Street and, fearing a commotion, I had gone inside to summon the other bears.

'Where was Mr Rowland at this time?' Heron asked.

He was inside the theatre selling tickets.

'Did he come out at any time?'

Only after the disturbance was over. Then he helped those who had been injured into a lower room in the theatre, and offered them free tickets to the opera to compensate them for their maltreatment.

'Can you tell me how Mr Rowland was dressed at this time?'

He was wearing his usual clothes for these performances: a black coat and black pantaloons reaching to the ankle in the new style.

'During the disturbance, did you see anyone strike the deceased?'

I saw a mob armed with wooden clubs assault our customers without the least provocation. In the crowd, I could not see who was being struck, but among the assailants I could see Messrs Oates, Slider and Mugger, all of whom are in this court – I extended a paw to indicate them – *and also Mr Daniel Mendoza, who is not present today.*

Pike was on his feet, spluttering, 'This is hearsay evidence, Your Honour, and without confirmation.'

The judge asked, 'Mr Heron, can you substantiate these allegations?'

'I can, your Honour, and my next witness shall demonstrate their truth.'

Pike did not try to cross-examine me: I think he was afraid of what I would write on my board for all to see. The next witness was someone I had not seen before, or at least had not noticed: a Mr Roylance Allman, who had been among those waiting outside the theatre to buy a ticket. His testimony exactly matched my own, with the addition that he had been struck by Daniel Mendoza himself, whose face is well known to the public after his career as a prizefighter.

In his final speech, Mr Heron was at pains to point out the inadequacy of the evidence of the prosecution witnesses – he did not utter the word 'lies', but it was there, hanging in the air for all to see. He pointed out that Mrs Fairbrother had 'misremembered' the details of Fred's clothing, and that she could hardly have attended the performance, as there is no scene in which a god descends. He offered to show the jury the libretto of the opera, which they declined. We were feeling modestly hopeful when the jury retired, and the court adjourned.

They were back within ten minutes, though it took another ten for the returning crowd to settle down and take their places. I noticed that Oates, Slider, Mugger and Mrs Fairbrother were not among those who came back.

'Members of the jury,' said Mr Justice Gaunt, 'have you considered your verdict?'

'We have, Your Honour,' replied the foreman. He was looking most uncomfortable, as were they all, and said no more.

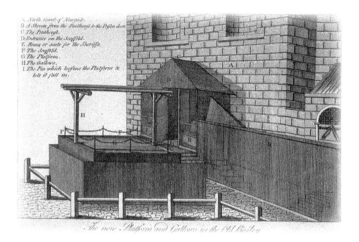

'Out with it, man,' said the judge.

'Your honour, we find the accused … *guilty* … of murder.'

A gasp of horror resounded through the crowded court. Even the judge was visibly astonished. 'And is that the verdict of you all?'

'Er, it is, Your Honour.'

Directing a contemptuous glare at the venal wretch, the judge reluctantly reached for his black cap, a little square of silk resting on a cushion, and laid it on top of his full-bottomed wig. He said heavily, 'Then I have no other course. Prisoner at the bar, you have been found guilty of murder. The sentence of the court is that you shall be taken from here to a place of execution, and there hanged by the neck until you are dead.' He looked regretfully at Fred, who had collapsed against the wall of the dock. 'And may the Lord have mercy on your soul.'

Fred, barely conscious, was carried out of the court by two burly officers. We could hardly stand ourselves, and reeled into the street.

Jem was the first to rally. 'Me dear ole bears,' he said. 'We all knows the jury was nobbled. It 'appens. But we ain't 'avin' this, no way. We're agoin' to get 'im out.'

14.

Fred is to be hanged on Monday the 23rd – a perilously short date. We
have been conferring as to how to contrive his rescue. Jem was in favour
of blowing down the front door with a charge of gunpowder brought
in on a handcart, followed by an invasion of bears to overwhelm the
gaolers and release not only Fred, but all the prisoners. A wonderful
dream, but alas! hardly feasible. A glance at the massive stone front
designed by George Dance, with its menacing carved fetters above a
tiny doorway heavily armed with iron, shows that it would be unlikely
to fall to anything short of a sustained artillery barrage, something that
might attract unwelcome attention in a London street.

I had a subtler idea. *Do you remember,* I wrote on my slate, *the rescue of the Earl of Nithsdale after the 1715 Rebellion?*

'No,' said Jem. 'Never 'eard of 'im. Do tell.'

He was imprisoned in the Tower, and due to be executed the following morning. He was rescued by his wife. She was allowed to visit him and wish him a last farewell. She went in accompanied by her maid, who concealed under her skirts a second dress identical with her own. In the Tower, they dressed the Earl in these clothes, and Lady Nithsdale left with him behind her, keeping out of the direct gaze of the guards. (I could also have mentioned Polyaenus' account of how King Theopompus of Sparta escaped from an Arcadian prison dressed in the female clothes his wife Queen Chilonis had brought him.)

'But,' Jem, said, 'that left the maid inside. 'Ow'd they get 'er out without blowin' the gaff?'

That was the cleverest part of the scheme. Soon after the Earl escaped, the guard was changed. The maid went out past the new guard, who did not know how many people had gone in. Since she was obviously a girl, she was not suspected.

'I think we got a plan,' said Jem. 'Well done, Daisy me dear, we thought yer'd come up with somethin'. But they know Fred ain't got a wife, and where do we find a gal?'

Do you think we could pay Dolores O'Connor to help us? She badly needs some money, and she has no love to Kemble and his bravoes.

'Mebbe.'

She could pretend to be his daughter, and you could escort her in and leave with Fred.

'That's it,' said Jem. 'Not bad at all, me ole Daisy. What would we do without yer? We'll do it on Sunday evening when they're drunk, an' that gives us two days to get ready.'

Can you find out when the guard changes?

'O' course. They drinks at an inn just down the street.'

I wish we could do this at once, and not leave poor Fred in agony for two more days. But Jem's choice of a time is sensible, and we must prepare our assault thoroughly.

'Whatever 'appens, we're agoin' to be on the run,' said Jem. 'I best get down to the bank afore it shuts an' get out all our wedge.'

It was lucky that Fred had assigned Jem the power to deal with Cox's and King's. I wrote: *Can we do anything for the people at the theatre?*

'I'll 'ave a word with 'em. The place is only rented. 'Ope they'll be able to cope on their own with a new opera. But to be honest, without bears they ain't got much, 'ave they?'

Jem hurried off. Well, we have a plan, though a desperate one, and we are united in our determination to see it through. As Virgil wrote, *Quo res cunque cadent, unum et commune periclum, / Una salus ambolus erit,* However events may fall out, for us there will be one common danger, one source of safety.

October 21st, 1809.

We found Dolores miserably huddled in a doorway in Covent Garden. 'I couldn't even set up as a flower gal,' she said. 'They got a sort o' guild, an' if yer ain't in, yer out.'

Jem said, 'Yer 'elped us, an' we ain't forgettin' that. We'll look after yer no matter what, 'cos yer one of us now. But we do need yer 'elp again for one thing, and it's a mite tricky.' And he explained our plan, adding, 'Worst thing that can 'appen to yer, yer gets thrown out o' Newgate.'

'Better'n being thrown in, I reckon,' she said. 'I'm for it.'

'Lor' bless yer, me gal, yer a treasure.'

They went off together to buy two identical dresses. Fred is small and slight, and he would have no difficulty in getting into women's clothes, but he will have to conceal his face as he comes out. Desperate weeping into a handkerchief should be enough to work the deception.

Jem and Dolores spent the evening rehearsing our drama, with far greater earnestness than for some foolish romance about the imaginary loves of Vestal virgins. Dolores makes a fine show as a grief-stricken daughter, and Jem has only to be himself.

October 22ⁿᵈ, 1809.

I write this as we stand ready for action. And how we have prepared! In the words of Heliodorus, Τὰ μεγάλα τῶν πραγμάτων μεγάλων δεῖται κατασκευῶν, Great deeds need great preparations. Our first need after we have liberated Fred is a speedy escape, and for this, regardless of expense, we have hired two coaches each with four horses, which are now waiting for us in Warwick Lane on the corner of Newgate Street. We are taking as little as possible with is, but we shall require the means to sustain ourselves on our journey, wherever we may be bound, and we must take with us all the impedimenta of our various performances, including the fire-eating and sword-swallowing equipment and of course little Henry's Unirota. All these can be carried on foot in our packs when needful. We also have Fred and Jem's prized Baker rifles, and a sufficiency of powder, ball and spare flints for them.

The bears are assembled beside the coaches, ready to intervene should things not go as smoothly as we hope.

The guard at the prison is changed at six p.m. It is now a quarter past five, and Jem and Dolores are setting off on their perilous exploit. Jem carries nothing but a purse of golden guineas and a bag containing two bottles of brandy, but Dolores has an awkward load under her dress. We wisely chose a rather old-fashioned attire with a much fuller skirt than is the mode now, giving her the air of a simple country girl but also concealing a second dress, a lady's red wig the same colour as her own hair, a man's brown wig and a bag stuffed with sawdust the size of a man's head, whose use will be explained presently. It is hard for her to walk naturally, but she is pretending to be almost fainting with grief and clinging to Jem's shoulder.

Now I must put down my pen and ready us all for a hasty departure. I hope to be able to resume our tale later.

October 23ʳᵈ, 1809.

I now recount yesterday evening's events inside the gaol, as related to me by Jem. He and Dolores knocked at the gate, and some guineas changed hands, necessary lubricants for any activity in a prison. The guards accepted Jem's story that he had brought Fred's only daughter to bid her a last farewell, and she wept so copiously and sobbed so loudly that they must have been glad to leave the two of them alone in Fred's cell.

On the way up the stairs, Jem said to the escorting guard, 'We brought a couple o' bottles o' brandy to sweeten 'is last 'ours, like. But we'll only be needin' the one, I think, so yer might as well 'ave the other.' The guard needed no prompting to take it.

As they opened the cell, Dolores screamed, 'Daddy, me poor Daddy,' and flung herself into his arms, stifling any expression of surprise that he might have uttered.

Once the door was slammed behind them and the guard had clanked down the staircase, Dolores continued to sob theatrically while all engaged in frantic activity. A whispered explanation from Jem, and then Dolores was stripping off his clothes.

''E were blushin' like a beetroot,' she said. 'But I says to 'im, it ain't nothin' what I ain't seen before, me 'avin six brothers. We'll make a lovely lady o' yer, I says.'

While Dolores dressed him, Jem was making a dummy with Fred's own clothes stuffed with straw from the bedding. He arranged it on the

bed so that it faced the wall in an attitude of despair, adding the bag of sawdust and the brown wig for a head. Some artfully disposed straw masked its missing feet.

As soon as Fred was fully rigged out and equipped with a large cotton handkerchief to weep into and hide his unshaven face, it was ten to six and time to leave. Jem poured some of the bottle of brandy on to the bedding to make a spirituous reek, and then knocked loudly on the cell door to summon the guards, who were now looking distinctly fuddled after sharing a bottle of brandy, and not inclined to be too inquisitive.

''E's sleepin' now,' he said. ''Twould be a kindness to leave 'im be for a while, 'e ain't got much to look forrard to. An' yer might as well 'ave the rest o' 'is bottle, 'e won't be needin' it tomorrow, poor ole cove.'

As well as the bottle, two more guineas changed hands. The guards barely glanced at the weeping 'daughter', now sobbing vociferously into her handkerchief, and the two of them were soon down the staircase and out of the gate, amazed by their success. As Propertius astutely remarked, *Aurum omnes, victa iam pietate, colunt*, All worship gold, and decency is now completely overthrown.

I and the watching bears saw them come around the corner into Newgate Street, at once abandoning their previous demeanour as Fred rushed to meet us in an ungainly stride, clutching his unaccustomed skirts. It was a moment of joy – but not unmixed, as we still had to wait for the courageous Dolores to emerge.

The bells of various City clocks struck six in a ragged succession, and we were all consumed with anxious expectation. Then, at five minutes past the hour, we saw her red hair blazing at the corner. She broke into a run, and we bundled her into a coach and off we all galloped down Newgate Street and into Cheapside.

''Tweren't all that 'ard,' she said. 'I waited till I 'eard the new guards arrivin', an' then I banged on the door till they came. I weren't 'alf anxious to get out o' that place.' But I did a lot o' screechin' about me poor Daddy bein 'anged, an' they couldn't wait to be rid o'me.'

It was only a matter of time before the new guards would unmask the dummy on the bed, so we had to be off as fast as we could. Fortunately the law cannot keep up with a coach and four. We are not heading for Dover, the all too obvious road of escape. Jem knows some folk in Great Yarmouth, on the east coast, mainly a fishing town but with enough ships calling to give us an early chance of a passage – but to where, heaven only knows.

In the coach the astonished Fred, slowly rising from the depths of despair, recovered himself enough to say, 'Well, Daisy me dear, we're on the run again. We was always wanderin' folk, you an' me, an' I can't say as 'ow I dislikes that. Beats gettin' 'anged, any'ow.'

15.

We are at Romford in Essex, after a circuitous journey to throw pursuers off the scent. Our coaches crossed London Bridge as if bound for Dover, but instead we soon left the Kent Road and took the Woolwich ferry back across the river. By the time we were back on the north shore it was completely dark and we made little further progress, but at least we are in a place where the authorities are unlikely to find us. The horses will have a chance to rest overnight, and there will be no need to change them until we have gone some way tomorrow.

There is room for only four bears inside each coach, so little Henry has to sit beside a coachman, muffled in a waterproof cape with a hood. Dolores sits on the other side, her red hair streaming in the wind, so no one on the road notices anything else. Fred and Jem sit outside on the other coach. On each, a guard sits at the rear with a blunderbuss. We could have taken care of that ourselves, but must observe convention.

We are spending the night in a barn outside the town to avoid notice. The coachmen and guards insisted on being put up in an inn, at our expense of course. They have strict orders, sweetened with a modest payment, not to talk about their passengers, and I think they will hold their tongues as it would be to their disadvantage to be known to have aided an escaped prisoner.

October 26ᵗʰ, 1809.

We are in Great Yarmouth, a reasonably elegant town since it is now patronised by the gentry in quest of the sea bathing cure for their excesses. However, since the cold autumn winds have started to blow the fashionable folk are gone, and the place is given over to the Royal Navy, for which it serves as a supply base, and to a large fishing fleet.

It has not been a quick journey, as we have travelled on small roads in bad condition for much of the way. We spent the previous night at Ipswich. The only notable incident during that day was the loss of a wheel near Colchester, but luckily the coach was not overset and the fault was quickly corrected when four bears held up the axle for the wheel to be returned to its place and secured with a new pin. Our destination is the Bugle Inn in the Market Square, the usual stopping place of this coach when visiting Yarmouth.

As we approached the town we were disagreeably surprised to see the wooden frames of a naval semaphore telegraph set up along the road, on church towers and on such hills as can be found in this flat countryside. It seems that the line was completed last year, and now a message can pass between London and Yarmouth in minutes. However, it is used only for naval communications, and the civil authorities cannot avail themselves of it except perhaps in the direst emergency. We do not think that Fred's escape would be counted as such.

This semaphore system was devised by Lord George Murray. It uses six shutters, and can be operated at night by placing lamps behind each of the shutters. Thirty-two different combinations are

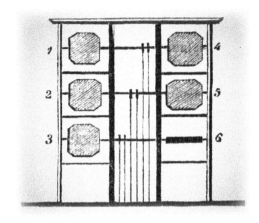

possible, permitting transmission of all the letters of the alphabet as well as a few extra codes to indicate the start and finish of messages, readiness to send and receive, and the beginning and end of numeric codes.

I consider it unnecessarily complicated, since it would be possible to send messages with a single shutter that could be opened or closed at a constant rate set by identical pendulums in each station. Instead of frantically manipulating all the levers of six shutters, you could simply move one six times.

But while I was musing on such matters, danger presented itself from another direction. We were now in the streets of Yarmouth, and the coach with Fred and Jem travelling outside was at the front, with myself inside. There was a thump, and I saw Fred on the ground and racing away into a side street; a moment later Jem followed him.

A glance out of the window revealed the reason. A squad of Marines was approaching us, muskets at the ready, escorting a sullen rabble of yokels. It was the press gang, exercising their infamous right to seize men from the streets and forcibly enlist them in the navy.

The coachmen and guards, unable to desert their posts, were quickly surrounded, the guards' blunderbusses of no avail against twenty muskets and the force of an unjust law. They were obliged to descend and join the captive band.

Dolores, of course, was in no danger, though her fury was something to behold. While she raged against the Marines in words that I blush to remember, they were pointing their weapons at little Henry, disguised in his hooded coat. When he pushed back his hood and they found a small bear staring at them with naked hostility they were amazed, but this was nothing to their astonishment when they forced open the doors of the coaches and found eight more bears. They beat a hasty retreat.

Having lost our coachmen, all we could do was continue to the Bugle, leading the horses as we have no coach-driving skills. Here Dolores explained events to an agent, who was wearily unsurprised – such things seem to happen all too often here – and simply said that he would have to enlist more coachmen and guards, if the press gang had left any, before looking for passengers for the return journey.

Angelina, who had detached herself from the party and followed the scent of Fred and Jem to their hiding place in a timber yard, now came to the inn, and we followed her back to meet them. 'First thing we got to do,' said Fred, 'is to get out o' this Godforsaken town and on to the water.'

October 27th, 1809.

The first ship to leave Yarmouth is the *Wensleydale*, bound for St Petersburg with a cargo of port and cheap brass samovars made in Birmingham. She is short-handed. 'Why not?' said Fred. 'I ain't never bin to Russia, and they does say as 'ow travel broadens the mind.'

Russia must be a fine country for bears, and we were happy to agree. We asked Dolores whether she wanted to travel with us, offering her some money to live on if she stayed. She has decided to come, and we are all delighted – especially Jem. I sense that there is a growing tenderness between them.

The captain, one Gideon Larkspur, had heard of our exploit in bringing a ship from the Bay of Biscay to Portsmouth with a crew of just nine bears, and took us on as able seamen and sea bears without asking for certificates (which we do not have). Dolores is engaged as a cook.

October 29th, 1809.

It is good to be afloat again. Bears may not be born to roam the ocean but, as Plautus says, *Mare quidem commune certus est omnibus,* The sea is surely common to us all. Fred is now fully recovered from his ordeal, and on our first evening he struck up a merry gavotte on his flute and we all danced. He followed it with a hornpipe in which the sailors joined.

Yesterday a gale blew up, and we astounded the crew with the celerity with which we shortened sail. The samovars, packed in straw in wooden crates, have worked loose, and every time the ship rolls there is an outburst of clattering and clanging in addition to the usual groans, rattles and thumps of a ship at sea.

November 5ᵗʰ, 1809 (October 24ᵗʰ Old Style).

We have arrived in St Petersburg, only to find that we have gained twelve days on our voyage. The Russians still use the old Julian calendar which we in England abandoned in 1752, and for them it is the 24th of October, the day when we were galloping around Essex trying to shake off our pursuers. But in both countries it is Sunday, and we must wait until tomorrow before we can start unloading our cargo.

Having nothing much to do, we went ashore and explored the city. It is laid out on a grand scale: the public buildings are magnificent and the churches ornate to a degree that we in England forgot after the Middle Ages. But when you pass beyond the centre, the fine show vanishes and there is little but wooden shacks, while the broad paved roads dwindle into muddy tracks that soon fade away in the virgin forest.

This suited us well. We found an abandoned and partly ruined cabin and made makeshift repairs to the roof with pine branches. It is already snowing, and a layer of snow on the roof will serve to make it weatherproof for now. There was a stove in good enough order to be used, and we have kindled a merry blaze which keeps us snug and warm.

November 6th, 1809 (October 25th O.S.).

It is the fourth anniversary of my fateful meeting with Lord Byron. How much has changed in this time! I have been a student, a soldier and an impresario, and have gained much experience of life. As Solon said, Γηράσκω δ' αιεὶ πολλὰ διδασκόμενος, I grow old ever learning many things.

We spent the day unloading the cargo of the *Wensleydale*. While the bears hauled crates out of the hold, a cordon of sailors maintained a guard around the growing pile of merchandise to keep out as best they could the hordes of scallywags and ragamuffins eager to snatch a bottle of port or a samovar from its crate.

Fred, Jem and Dolores have had to buy winter clothing: heavy woollen coats, hats of rabbit fur, mittens and fleece-lined boots – quite an expense. We bears, of course, laugh at the Russian chill.

In the evening we repaired to an inn, thinking that we might perform and earn a little ready cash – we are by no means destitute, but a genteel sufficiency is always agreeable. However, when we arrived there was already a dancing bear, chained in the cruel old style while his keeper stamped around with a great wooden stave. The spectacle, so long forgotten, seared all our hearts, but there was little we could do. One cannot simply charge in and abduct a bear by force.

As I write this journal, I am interrupted. It is the Russian bear, trailing a length of chain which he has broken by main force. He has tracked us down to our cabin.

We are welcoming him as only bears can, and while we are feeding him with some of our bag of hares and grouse shot by Fred, Jem is cutting off his shackles with a hacksaw. His name is Arkady. We are uncertain what to do, as we are not on the march as when we adopted Angelina, and his owner will be looking for him.

November 7ᵗʰ, 1809 (October 26ᵗʰ O.S.).

We decided that we must take the matter into our own hands before we were accused of abducting Arkady. Accordingly, Fred and Jem went to the inn where he had been dancing, and soon found the bear's owner. Fortunately he spoke a little French, as does Fred, and while their differing accents and vocabularies made communication slow they did not entirely impede it. He is called Alexey. They conducted him back to our cabin, where he found ten bears confronting him with a gaze that was not entirely friendly. Thus disadvantaged, he was obliged to bargain.

We began our negotiations with a dance. Jem played a stately sarabande on his flute, and my own dear Bruin and Angelina glided through its intricate evolutions with ineffable grace. He followed it with a lively gigue, and mercurial gaiety pervaded the cabin. Alexey watched open-mouthed.

Then Fred said to him simply – very simply in his halting French – 'Alexey, you see what bears can do. We can teach your bear to dance like that. But no more chains, not never, no more sticks. Your bear is your colleague, your companion, your friend. Will you stay with us and we will teach him?'

Alexey, still dumbfounded by what he had seen, could say nothing but '*Da.*'

While Arkady is being educated, Alexey will act as our guide to a new and unfamiliar land. He is not a bad man. He simply did not understand that bears are rational beings and do not belong to people. The spectacle of a band of bears living in freedom and harmony with three humans whom, had they wished to, they could have torn to pieces in an instant, has opened his eyes. They have been further opened by the realisation that, with a bear who dances beautifully, he can earn more roubles than he had ever dreamed of.

November 11ᵗʰ, 1809 (October 30ᵗʰ O.S.).

Alexey is teaching us the *gopak*, a dance traditionally performed by Ukrainian soldiers. It is a fine spectacle but strains the knees of humans and bears alike.

He plays a peculiar triangular guitar with three strings, which is called a *balalaika*. With Jem's flute and Fred's fiddle we have an orchestra of sorts, and what they lack in finesse they make up for in panache. Dolores is now joining in some of our dances, to great effect.

Tutored by Alexey, the three humans are now able to speak a little Russian. Fred has found me a tattered Russian-Latin dictionary and a Russian grammar, and I am learning to write the language. The alphabet is easy enough, having been adapted from Greek by St Cyril and St

Methodius in the ninth century by the addition of a few extra letters. The grammar is less easy: for example, nouns, in additional to the usual nominative, accusative, genitive and dative cases, have instrumental and prepositional cases, while some nouns add the vocative and locative (familiar enough from Latin), the partitive (a kind of alternative genitive) and the caritive (which negates the meaning of the word). But we bears make light of such complications.

November 15ᵗʰ, 1809 (November 3ʳᵈ O.S.)

We considered our new performance well enough rehearsed, and went into the city to see how it would fare. The cold weather makes it harder to find a space to perform, for the patrons of inns are all crowded indoors and no one is in the yard. But, as we neared the centre of the city, we passed by the lighted windows of one of the fashionable establishments now known by the French name of *café* – though they are much finer than the coffee houses we knew in London. Its front gave on to a spacious square, swept clear of snow by serfs. Fred was struck by inspiration. 'Let's do the show right here,' he said.

So our little band struck up a merry tune, and we bent all our energies to the dance. Dolores capered prettily in the centre, hatless, her red hair flying. By the time we started to perform the *gopak*, the windows were lined with elegantly dressed people, and they were beginning to trickle out of the door for a better view. We finished to rapturous applause and cheering, and several hats passed around the crowd gathered a harvest of roubles.

As Dolores was donning her coat and the men were putting away their instruments, a finely attired gentleman approached Fred and addressed him in French, asking who we were. Fred replied that we were an English company on tour (which sounded better than 'fugitives from the law') and that we had performed before His Royal Highness the Prince of Wales (which was perfectly true). The man said, 'I believe that his Imperial Majesty Aleksandr, Tsar of All the Russias, would be graciously pleased to witness your performance. Would you be kind enough to give me your address?'

16.

This morning a gorgeously attired equerry from the palace cantered up to our tumbledown shack on a shining black horse to deliver a wafer of thick cream-coloured pasteboard with gilt edges. It bore a message, fortunately in French as our Russian is not yet what it might be. We are *commanded* to attend His Imperial Majesty forthwith. Emperors do not invite, or suggest that it might be convenient to attend. And no answer is required, save that of humble compliance.

We packed our meagre effects, and off we trooped to the Winter Palace. It is an imposing building, not lofty – just three storeys high –

but its front, bedecked with statues and urns, is so long that it stretches into the distance. We were directed to a lowly side entrance, where we were greeted by a gentleman who introduced himself as Grigory Putin, the Imperial Director of Music. From his demeanour, we infer that he directs much more than music, and in this uncertain place we are anxious to be on his side.

Today is Thursday, and we are to perform before the Emperor on Saturday – scant time for rehearsal, but after our travels we are accustomed to readying a show in haste to suit the circumstances. It transpires that the court orchestra has parts for *La Vestale*, brought directly from Paris, and we have agreed that its closing ballet shall be the main event in our performance. It will be preceded by a series of English, Spanish and Portuguese dances interspersed with acrobatic intermezzi performed with our talented troupe, and followed by a *gopak* to round off the evening with a fitting tribute to our Russian hosts.

Having left England in haste we have no suitable costumes, but with a wave of his hand Putin summoned a throng of imperial seamstresses, and they are stitching away as I write. Jem is deep in consultation with the orchestra, and Fred, ever practical, is arranging the rigging for Peter and Emily's slack rope performance, and ensuring that no readily combustible draperies will hang too close to Bruin's fire-eating act. I do not think that the imperial theatre will ever have witnessed anything like the fare that we plan to give them.

November 18th, 1809 (November 6th O.S.).

I write this after our performance – and what a performance! It was a triumph compared to which our show at Carlton House before the Prince of Wales was a mere fairground turn. The bears, gorgeously bedecked, danced and balanced and ate fire with a verve and dash that had the audience on their feet cheering louder and louder after every episode. Little Henry's performance on the Unirota, which he rode up and down the aisle while juggling with five jewelled eggs borrowed from the treasury, had them gasping. After the final *gopak*, dukes and duchesses besieged the stage to garland us with flowers.

When the applause had subsided, everyone trooped off to a reception in the state rooms of the palace. They are of unexampled magnificence, putting the motley residences of the English court to shame.

The courtiers were dripping with diamonds and rubies which, I am informed, can be picked up at the roadside in Siberia (though privately I suspect that the gathering is done by an army of serfs while an overseer stands over them with a great *knout,* a scourge with metal weights on each tongue). The courtiers are also drenched in perfume and, looking at it from the human point of view, they need it. To a bear's more sensitive nose, the principal scent is that of unwashed humanity, overlaid with a discordant welter of musk and castor, ambergris and spikenard, and attar of roses and other floral extracts.

The palace itself, for all its glitter, is far from clean and all kinds of filth can be found in the corners. This, perhaps, is the essence of the Russian court: a shining facade of Frenchified elegance over a rough base reeking of the shaggy folk from the steppes. We bears can well understand this, as we too are superimposing our courtly dances on our natural behaviour – though we do it with greater grace and certainly greater cleanliness.

As I was musing on these matters, a splendidly attired nobleman approached Fred with a cry of 'Knock knock, me ole cock sparrer! I 'eard as 'ow some English coves 'ad turned up 'ere wiv bears an' all. An' wot brings yer to 'Oly Russia, 'f I m'y be so bold as ter arst?' He introduced himself as Count Bagarov, but we were all gasping at his mode of speech. Fred and Jem have the accents of ordinary Londoners, but he sounded as if he had been born in a thieves' den near the docks.

Fred managed to say, ''Onoured to meet yer, Yer

Serenity.' (I blessed my foresight in teaching him the modes of address for the various ranks of the Russian aristocracy.) 'We came 'ere in a bit of an 'urry, I 'as to confess. Things was gettin' a bit borin' like at 'ome.' (By which he meant 'dangerous'.)

'Ow, yer runnin', eh? Wot yer bin done fer?'

Fred explained with as much dignity as he could summon that he had been falsely accused of murder and condemned to death, but had been rescued at the last minute by his loyal companions.

'So yer was sprung jest afore yer was ter dangle, eh? Yer got some fly foxes wiv yer, an' no mistake.'

I will give the rest of this conversation in *oratio obliqua*, as it is becoming wearisome to transcribe their peculiar mode of speech. Yet let us heed the proverb cited by Apostolius, Ἀγροίκου μὴ καταφρόνει ῥήτορος, Despise not a rustic speaker.

Fred congratulated the Count on his fluent command of English, and the Count explained that he had been brought up by an English nursemaid born in Bow, who had come to St Petersburg with some London merchants to care for an infant who had perished of the measles, after which she had summarily been cast adrift. The old Count had rescued her and charged her with the rearing of his little son, which she had done admirably and, in her old age, was still residing at their residence in Archangel on the shores of the White Sea.

The Count now disclosed that he had approached Fred for a purpose. The family had acquired a polar bear cub whose mother had been shot by hunters, and had determined to bring him up as a pet. (At this, all the bears pricked up their ears to hear the rest of the story. None of us has ever seen one of these famous white bears, and indeed some dismiss them as mythical creatures.) All went well for a while, the Count said, but the bear, whose name is Boris, is now almost fully grown and is chafing in confinement. He cannot be returned to the polar waste as, without experience, he would soon perish; but he is ill suited to be treated like a lapdog in the house of a nobleman. He has become moody and occasionally violent, and nearly killed one of his devoted keepers.

Would we, the Count asked, come to Archangel with him before the approaching winter made the roads impassable, and see what we could do to relieve Boris's sad plight? Fred glanced around at a circle of bears and humans nodding in assent. Not only are we coming to the aid of a fellow bear, we are securing ourselves a comfortable home for the northern winter, a season whose rigours drive even the hardiest bears to hibernate in a snowy shelter. As Horace wrote, *Bruma recurrit iners*, The sluggish winter returns.

At this point our conversation was interrupted by an equerry with a message from the Tsar himself. His Imperial Majesty commanded us to attend him on Monday morning, in two days' time. Of course we had no idea of the purpose of this summons, but Fred had the presence of mind to explain to the functionary that our command of French was less than perfect – which was all too obvious – and to ask if Count Bagarov could be summoned to act as an interpreter where needed, something that our new friend was happy to do, understandably wishing to be seen as useful to his sovereign.

November 19th, 1809 (November 7th O.S.).

We have spent Sunday at the palace in grand style, accommodated, bears and humans alike, in splendid apartments with lackeys at our beck and call. Accustomed to instant obedience, they did not bat an eyelid when Fred asked them to bring forty pounds of raw meat for our sustenance. It was horse, and none the worse for that.

We attended divine service in the palace chapel. The structure is spacious and sumptuously decorated with shining golden mosaics, and the vocal music was of strange and wondrous beauty, but the order of service was most unexpected. The congregation takes no part in the proceedings, remaining standing and wandering around the edges of the chapel, while the worship is conducted by clerics in a high-walled pen in the middle, almost screened from view, though at one point the Host is raised to cries of acclamation. The rite is in the old Church Slavonic language, absolutely incomprehensible to all present. I prefer our English Matins, where one feels that one has some part in the proceedings.

November 20th, 1809 (November 8th O.S.).

This morning we had an audience with the Tsar. We had no idea of why he wanted to speak with us, except perhaps to examine a curiosity that had arrived in his land; but we soon found out.

There were fourteen of us: the ten bears, Fred, Jem, Dolores and Count Bagarov. We were ushered into the imperial presence and bowed in what we hoped was an acceptable manner. Dolores managed a tidy curtsey, which she had spent some time practising the previous evening.

The Tsar motioned us to a large table, where he sat on one side and the other humans took chairs on the other, while the bears sat on the floor in decorous and attentive attitudes. The conversation was conducted in French, with occasional assistance from the Count when Fred could not find the right word – but I will not tire you with details, and will simply report the bare bones of the matter.

The Tsar first addressed Fred: 'I have heard that you fought the French in Spain and Portugal.'

Fred indicated that this was true.

'Would you then give me your opinion of the French as a fighting force?'

Fred replied, 'Sire, we were up against Soult, and he is a fine general and nearly had us more than once. But two things saved us. First, we were fighting with the population, and he was fighting against them,

and so we were able to raise a local band of irregulars who harassed his troops quite effectively, with our aid if I may say so.' He waved his arm to encompass our band of fighting bears, who had indeed dismantled many a French soldier. 'And second, we have a general who can beat Soult at his own game, by which I mean Sir Arthur Wellesley. I believe that, in the long run of this conflict, Wellesley will out-general Soult and Ney and anyone that Napoleon can find to oppose him.'

The Tsar then turned to me. 'Daisy, I have heard that you are a bear well read in the classical historians, and I would like to hear your views of this conflict.'

I took up my slate and wrote in French, *Sire, I have indeed studied the works of Herodotus, Thucydides, Xenophon, Julius Caesar, Agricola, Suetonius and later authors such as Ammianus Marcellinus. But, if I may venture to make an enquiry that may be indiscreet, I believe that at present you have a formal alliance with Napoleon under the Treaty of Tilsit, and that my humble but honestly expressed views may not be favourable to that agreement.*

The Tsar replied, 'That, my dear bear, is exactly why I wished to canvass your opinion. Please speak freely.'

I wrote, *Then, Sire, I have this to say. I do not believe that any alliance with Napoleon is to be depended on. Napoleon has one aim, and that aim is conquest. He desires Spain, the German and Italian states, the Low Countries, Poland and Britain as part of his empire, and I think that before long he will tear up the treaty and turn his envious eyes on Russia. And when he does, it will be his undoing. I hesitate to invoke your namesake, Alexander of Macedon …*

'No, no, go on,' said Alexander of Russia.

… but he will make the same mistake. It is one thing to command an all-conquering army, and another to hold the lands that the army has conquered. I

believe that if Alexander had not died suddenly in Babylon, he would have seen his conquests vanish in his lifetime. He went too far; they could not be sustained. I believe that Napoleon, in his mad dream of ruling the world, will invade your country with a huge army under able generals, and perhaps will penetrate it for many hundreds of miles. But the farther he goes, the longer and more vulnerable his lines of supply will be. He will be defeated by two things: the ever lengthening distance between his forces and home, and another force against which there can be no winning …

'And what is that?'

… the Russian winter. It is something of which he has no knowledge, and for which he is completely unprepared. With General Winter on your side, you are assured of victory.

'Daisy,' replied the Tsar, 'your wise words have given me much to ponder. I thank you, and I thank Fred, for your counsel. I hear that you are to spend our mighty Russian winter with the good Count Bagarov, and if I need further advice I shall summon you again to St Petersburg. For now, you are dismissed, and I wish you a pleasant sojourn in Archangel.'

We all bowed and backed reverently out of the imperial presence, trying not to knock over the furniture.

17.

Count Bagarov was delighted by our reception by the Tsar. From an obscure minor courtier lurking in the corners of the state rooms of the Winter Palace, he has advanced to being regarded as a power behind the throne, able to marshal a band of seasoned warriors and learned bears to influence royal policy – or so he believes, and we do not wish to disillusion him. But he is still anxious to leave the court and return to his estates around Archangel. And why not? As Fred said, ''E knows 'ow to quit when 'e's winnin'.'

Marshal St Arnaud

He plans to depart tomorrow, and we shall go with him. We shall part company with Boris the bear and his human Alexey. They have decided to travel south for the winter, through Prussia and Austria, seeking the generous warmth of Italy where Fred and I spent many happy days. On Fred's advice, Alexey is planning to enlist a she-bear to give Boris a dancing partner and companion.

We have taught them all we know about dancing, and with Alexey's help our command of Russian is now moderate, but most importantly Boris is now a happy bear who dances for his own pleasure and that of an appreciative audience. It has been a fruitful exchange.

November 22nd, 1809 (November 10th O.S.).

This is a country without proper roads, and to travel from St Petersburg to Archangel as the northern winter tightens its grip is no easy task. It could be accomplished by sea, but that would be a slow southward voyage down the Baltic and back northwards around the whole length of Norway and the north coast of Finland; and a storm where the North Atlantic meets the Arctic Ocean is something no sensible person would wish to endure. Or we could sail up the Gulf of Bothnia to Kemi, cut across the neck of Finland to Kandalaksha, and again take ship to cross the White Sea to Archangel – but that would be a complicated and wearisome detour.

So we must go by land, on a convoy of sleighs drawn by three horses – the Russian term for this unusual arrangement is *troika*. The roads, barely passable in summer, are now icy tracks marked only by stakes driven into the frozen ground, and they snake circuitously between a myriad of lakes large and small, their surfaces now frozen but treacherous to venture across. The distance in a straight line is a mere 300 miles, but the road is far from straight.

Rather than skirt the western edge of Lake Ladoga, whose numerous inlets require slow ferry crossings, on our first day we have travelled north-west on a relatively straight road to Vyborg, from where we can turn north-east towards our destination. Difficult as the journey is in many ways, I have to say that the even glide of a sleigh over the snow is vastly more comfortable than the bruising jolting of a coach on the stones and potholes of an English road. The frail humans are warmly wrapped in sheepskins, and we bears ride our vehicles comfortable in our own fur and exulting in the bracing chill.

The journey is not without its hazards. As we neared our first day's destination, a single sleigh raced by us in the opposite direction, pursued by wolves snapping at the horses, while a man desperately but all too infrequently discharged his pistol against them – is there no way of

devising a method of reloading these crude weapons more quickly? It was a lucky encounter for them. When the bears leapt into the snow, most of the wolves fled with their tails between their legs. Those that did not provided us with a nutritious if stringy supper.

We passed the night in a simple inn, no worse than many in England. It is amusing to travel with a nobleman who demands the best of everything and has money to pay for it, only to find that there is little on offer. But there was plenty of the fiery Russian spirit called *vodka*, and the evening was a merry one with music and dancing.

November 30th, 1809 (November 18th O.S.).

We are arrived in Archangel, or Arkhangel'sk as it is properly called in Russian (the apostrophe represents the Cyrillic letter ь, which is not pronounced and merely indicates that the previous consonant should be pronounced lightly). Once an important port often visited by mainly Dutch traders, the city is sadly decayed as most Russian trade now goes through the Baltic and St Petersburg.

As we paused to view the prospect from the waterfront, we were approached by a thin, mean-looking man who, to our surprise, addressed

us in English – no doubt he had heard us speaking in that language. He introduced himself as John Bellingham, and told us that he had recently been imprisoned in Archangel and, although now set at liberty, was forbidden to leave the city.

He then launched into a circuitous and fantastic tale of woe about a lost Russian ship called the *Soleure*, which he suggested had been deliberately sunk to perpetrate a fraud upon its insurers. He had, it seems, repeated this accusation to the authorities again and again until he had made himself so obnoxious to them that he had been thrown into prison to keep him quiet. He was, he claimed, destitute and starving, and implored us for help in the lengthiest and most pathetic of terms. As Appian well remarked, Αἴ τε γὰρ συμφοραὶ ποιοῦσι μακρολόγους, Calamities make great talkers.

Count Bagarov drew Fred, Jem and me aside and said, 'Dunno wot yer fink, gents, but I reckons as 'ow this cove is a rum gagger an' tryin' ter rook us.'

'Me too,' said Fred. 'But why are they keepin' 'im 'ere if 'e's such a nuisance?'

'Tell yer wot I'll do,' Bagarov said. 'I knows the mayor, 'e's a square cove, a toppin' feller. Fink I'll nip in 'ere' – he indicated a large building, evidently the city hall – 'an' 'ave a word wiv 'im. Yer wait fer me in that ale-'ouse over there, an' I'll be back in two shakes o' a lamb's tail.' And off he strode. If you are a count, you do not need an appointment to speak with the mayor.

Sure enough, within half an hour, as we were enjoying some excellent Russian ale spoilt only by Bellingham's continued whining, he returned smiling. 'There's a ship bound fer England in the 'arbour now, the *Sara Louise*,' he said to Bellingham, 'an' yer on it, matey.' So get packin' yer bags, and never say as 'ow we didn' 'elp yer.'

Bellingham, with effusive thanks, scuttled off to our considerable relief. Bagarov told us that he had convinced the mayor that, whatever Bellingham's game was, he would only cause more trouble if he was detained in the city, and the wisest course of action was to get rid of him. But I fear that Archangel's gain will be England's loss, and that this miserable creature will cause trouble wherever he goes.

December 2ⁿᵈ, 1809 (November 20ᵗʰ O.S.).

We are now settled in Count Bagarov's substantial and well appointed residence on the outskirts of the city, and have had our first meeting with Boris the polar bear, for whose sake we have undertaken this long journey – though to be honest, it has been a most agreeable excursion.

Boris is housed in the stables, and has a spacious yard in which to exercise himself. He has food aplenty and a far easier life than that of a wild bear in the barren wastes, but he is certainly not happy. When we entered his enclosure he reared up in fury, and even we were alarmed by this great white creature brandishing his formidable claws. But when he saw little Henry looking at him with the innocence of a cub, he dropped back on to all fours and allowed us to approach him. For all his difference of colour he is a bear like us, and he will soon understand that we have come to relieve his solitude and, we earnestly hope, find him a purpose in life.

Jem played his flute and we danced. Boris was amazed. These things simply do not happen on the Arctic ice. Count Bagarov was with us, and in his countenance I saw the dawn of hope that his beloved bear will eventually find happiness in his enforced exile.

On my request, we brought Boris into the house for dinner: a copious supply of elk for us bears, and all kinds of Frenchified fal-lals for the humans, which we did not envy. But we were happy to share their Bordeaux, a drink fit for gods and bears. At lesser times the ordinary drink here is a kind of small beer called *kvass*, made by fermenting stale bread. It is palatable enough but feeble stuff for those accustomed to hearty English ale.

I am writing this in the stables, to which all the bears have returned to be with Boris. He is slightly fuddled with wine, and confused by being admitted to the house, but utterly content perhaps for the first time in his life, and has fallen asleep with his white head resting on Angelina's brown shoulder.

December 20th, 1809 (December 8th O.S.).

We have settled into the life of a Russian household in winter – though not the life of a wild Russian bear in winter for, having a warm place to spend our nights, we feel no need to hibernate. By day we range with Boris in the trackless forest, often bringing down an elk for a feast. And sometimes we dine in Count Bagarov's house, eating *kulebiaka*, a kind of sturgeon pie, with a knife and fork. Even Boris has learned the use of these ridiculous implements required by a species with weak teeth and the feeblest of claws, and it amuses us to deploy them in an elegant manner. In the evenings we dance, for our own delight and that of the household.

Beneath the rituals of civilisation, we are more happy living a bear's life, as the English members of our band are only now finding out. As Horace said, *Naturam expellas furca, tamen usque recurret*, You may drive out Nature with your fork, but soon enough she will come rushing back. Though he was speaking of an agricultural pitchfork rather than a table utensil unknown in his time, his words are still apt enough.

It was after one of our formal dinners, when we had all drunk deep of an excellent Georgian red wine and chased it down with aromatic Georgian brandy, that Count Bagarov felt free to disclose his secret aspiration. The company was speaking Russian, in which Fred, George and Dolores are now reasonably adept, so I will not tire your patience with an attempt to transcribe his peculiar command of English.

The Count said that he had long wished to return his home city of Archangel to the prosperity it had enjoyed as a port before the foundation of St Petersburg. He believed that to do this he should not look west, to trade with the nations of south-west Europe, now well served by way of the Baltic. Rather he should look eastwards. It was known, he said, that in the summer months when the Arctic ice had receded it was possible to sail along the northern coast of Russia, eventually reaching China and Japan and, by sailing south, the wealth of the East Indies and the spice islands of the Moluccas. This route, which we in England call the North-East Passage, had never been properly explored. It was time, the Count said, to try it.

Fred was clearly taken by the idea, but he felt bound to make a few observations. First, he said, he had spoken with sailors who had ventured some way into those regions, and there was always some ice, though not necessarily impassable. It would be necessary to use a vessel of particularly strong construction to avoid its being holed and sunk by ice floes, such as a bomb ship.

'What is a bomb ship?' asked the Count.

This was beyond Fred's Russian vocabulary to explain, so he reverted to English. 'It's a ship with big mortars for bombardin' forts from the sea. If you fired a mortar in an ordinary ship, it'd go through the bottom. So they're made extra thick all over.'

Second, Fred explained, even in summer it might be necessary to drive a ship at an ice sheet to break it and force a passage. With the wind in the Arctic, usually light and variable, it would be hard to do this. 'There's an American called Robert Fulton. 'E's made a boat driven by a steam engine – in fact two, one in America where it's doin' good business on a river, and another 'e made for the French when 'e was workin' for Napoleon. That one sank – what d'yer expect with Frenchies mannin' it? But 'e's shown that the thing works well enough, and you can forget about the way the wind's blowin'.'

'A capital idea,' said the Count in Russian, 'but I doubt we can tempt him to Arkhangel'sk, so we shall have to make do with what we have. At least we can try to find a bomb ship. I would like to make an expedition in spring, as soon as the ice has melted, and I hope that you will accompany me.'

'Yes!' said Fred and Jem and Dolores simply and in unison, and the bears roared assent.

18.

Count Bagarov has taken Fred's advice about using a bomb ship to penetrate the North-East Passage, and has sent one of his agents to St Petersburg to try to find such a vessel. This will be a long task, beginning with a slow overland journey, unprotected by bears, to the capital. Then a suitable ship has to be found in some Baltic port, and it must be paid for and manned, and lastly sailed round the coast of Norway and into the White Sea in the middle of an Arctic winter. At least, if and when the ship arrives, we shall know whether she is suitable for our venture.

The Count's enthusiasm for this expedition seems to be infinite, as indeed do his resources. We feel ourselves most fortunate to be taken up in this noble endeavour.

Christmas Day, 1809 (December 13th O.S.).

We are celebrating Christmas twice, first on our own day in the Gregorian calendar, then twelve days later in the Old Style Julian calendar – and why not? Our generous host is content with this arrangement, and his chaplain, Father Grigory, willingly arranged a service for us this morning, which was attended by all his household. It was conducted according to the customary and beautiful Orthodox rite, but the chaplain asked Fred to make a short address to the congregation to explain the reason for the service.

Fred in turn asked me to write it, and this is what I wrote.

My friends, we your English guests are celebrating Christmas twelve days before you simply because it is our custom, following human astronomers who have adjusted the calendar to correct the observations of other human astronomers. The date may be important to human and bears, but what is it in the mighty workings of Heaven? Indeed, it is one of the miracles of our religion that Christ was born not to a noble family who would have recorded the date, but to a humble carpenter's wife on an unknown day in an unknown year. He crept secretly into the world to save us not with a famous name that would have attracted many followers, but through private faith. In twelve days' time we shall be joining you to celebrate the birth of Christ once more, with all our hearts.

With the Count's help I translated this into Russian, and after Fred has delivered his address the Count repeated it in this language for the benefit of the congregation, who were visibly moved by its sentiments. There has long been a concord between the Anglican and Orthodox churches, based on the fact that we both have our differences with the Catholics.

In the evening we had a meal which was the nearest we could contrive to an English Christmas dinner. There were no roasted geese, but we had plenty of ptarmigans which in my view make better eating, and Dolores and the Count's cook had conspired to produce a very creditable Christmas pudding. The cook was astonished to discover that one can make a compact confection by boiling it in a buttered and floured cloth, and now has ideas of his own for Russian puddings. Perhaps this invention, which dates only from the sixteenth century, is England's greatest contribution to cookery.

We finished the evening with music and dancing, and Fred, Jem and Dolores sang English Christmas carols as well as they could, which were kindly received. But to tell the truth, I think that the Count's household think that we are quaint barbarians with outlandish customs. They are accommodating us generously, and we hope to repay them with all the help we can offer.

January 6th, 1810 (Christmas Day, 1809 O.S.)

Our feeble celebrations are looking very thin compared to the Orthodox Christmas. Festivities begin on Christmas Eve, with services in the chapel – long but never tiresome, with wonderful singing. Then there is a huge meal with twelve courses to represent the twelve Apostles, at which all kinds of strange foods appear, the principal one being *kutia*, a kind of wheat porridge with fruit, honey and poppy seeds which is probably not unlike the old English 'Christmas pottage' from the time before the English invention of the pudding cloth.

A long vigil in the chapel follows until midnight, when the proper celebration of the birth of Christ begins, with more services on Christmas Day followed by more feasting. Even a bear feels dazed by the alternation of divine services with copious food and drink. Both little Henry and Dolores had to be carried to their respective beds at the end of the proceedings, and I confess that I was a little unsteady myself.

January 7th, 1810 (December 26th, 1809 O.S.)

Jem has proposed to Dolores, and the two are to be married as soon as possible. Perhaps there is a certain urgency about this, as a bear's acute nose has been able to detect for some time that she is with child. Human decorum dictates that the niceties have to be observed, but it is much simpler for bears: you choose a mate with care but without celebration or contract, and you are together for life.

So far in this journal I have not mentioned my mate Silvio, the father of my dear cub Bruin, cruelly taken from me by a hunter's bullet when we

were touring in the Tyrol. Bruin and I and Fred will always feel the lack of his huge genial presence, and I shall never forget the joy of dancing with him in front of a cheering crowd to the thin music of Fred's fiddle. The Italian idea of 'hunting' is to kill everything in sight from sparrows upwards, a view all too common in the Mediterranean countries. I really only feel safe in England – or at least I did until recently, where the law has become a hunter crueller than any Italian with an ancient musket, driving us away to far Russia.

Father Grigory has kindly allowed the couple to be married there according to the Orthodox rite, which would not usually be permitted to foreigners but this is considered family business. It is a protracted proceeding, beginning with a celebration of betrothal in the entrance of the chapel, during which the couple held lighted candles. They also exchanged rings, something which in England is done at the wedding ceremony. All the liturgy is conducted in the Church Slavonic language, holy but incomprehensible even, I think, largely to the good priest himself. The bears looked on fondly, enjoying the sentiment for which it was worth enduring the lengthy ancient rigmarole.

February 11ᵗʰ, 1810 (January 31ˢᵗ O.S.)

This was the first day of the wedding celebration, which will continue for a week of feasting. It is a complicated business in this country, that is sure. It begins with a joke. The bridegroom arrives at the house of his bride – or in this case her room on the Count's house – in order to claim her by paying a 'bride price', a tradition which is mentioned by Homer, though he also speaks of a bride's family paying the more familiar dowry – the Iliad and Odyssey, assembled over some years, describe the traditions of several nations at different times.

The bride price is money or an article of jewellery; in Jem's case it was some gold sovereigns from the remnant of our meagre savings brought from England. The response was to bring out a veiled 'bride' who, when Jem lifted the veil, turned out to be Fred saying, 'Cheerio, me old mucker, yer'll 'ave to pay more to get the real gal.'

Jem accordingly threw in a few more sovereigns – not that it matters, as we are simply paying each other with money we hold in common – and a veiled Dolores was led out for examination and approval. The bears watched this bizarre exchange incredulously – we will never understand how humans manage to involve themselves in such machinations.

The couple then proceeded to the chapel, where the priest led them on to a square of carpet which looked light brown to a bear's eyes, but later Fred told me that it was rose-coloured to symbolise a rosy future. Here both Dolores and Jem were required to state publicly in Russian that they were marrying of their own free will, which they did prettily enough. After a good deal of Slavonic muttering, the priest put golden crowns – real enough and borrowed from the Count – on both their heads.

There followed an extraordinary procession in which the priest wrapped his stole around the joined hands of the couple and they all walked three times around the *analogion*, a lectern on which a copy of the Gospels was placed. Then there were more blessings, and the long proceedings finally closed.

This was followed by a lavish feast – the good Count does not stint his guests. We ate and drank and danced, and the humans sang. More than the gift of speech, which I can supply by writing on my slate, I envy humans their ability to sing melodiously rather than roaring tunelessly as we are constrained to do. And there are few nations that sing better than the Russians. The couple will wear their crowns until the festivities finish, with some difficulty as they have to be held on with one hand while dancing.

February 19th, 1810 (February 7th O.S.)

The long feast is finally over. I thought I would never get tired of eating and drinking, but I own that I am bloated and jaded with the effects of consuming gallons of *vodka*, a clean enough spirit when well made but every draught has its Nemesis. All the bears are looking worse for wear, and the humans are pale and dazed. But the important thing is that Jem and Dolores are now mates in the eyes of God, men and bears, and their headaches cannot mask their happiness.

March 1st, 1810 (February 16th O.S.)

I have not recently mentioned the recovery of Boris, the polar bear who is the newest recruit to our band. His spirits have been completely restored by good company and merriment, and indeed his wild hilarity is sometimes excessive, but polar bears are creatures of light and dark and not of the many shades of grey between. He joins in our dances with more enthusiasm than skill and, though we are all glad to have him with us, it is clear that he will never be a performer.

Sadly, he cannot remain with us for ever. Accustomed to the northern ice, he would be most uncomfortable in more southerly latitudes. Therefore Count Bagarov, always admirably solicitous of his people's needs, has been seeking a female polar bear to complete his life when we are gone. And, to our amazement, his agents seem to have found one.

In the *oblast* or province of Murmansk, separated from us by a few miles of sea, lives Turi, an ancient seer of the Sami people, whom the Swedes call Lapps. All his life he has dwelt in harmony with polar bears, which are sacred to the Sami, his latest companion being a she-bear no more than three years old, rescued as a cub after her parents were shot by Russian hunters.. He is now near the end of his days, but his bear will live on. Can we persuade her to cross the water to Archangel and a very different life in the company of an eccentric Russian noble, with a male bear that she has never seen before?

At least we can try to find out. As Ovid says, *Audentem Forsque Venusque iuvant*, Fortune and Love favour the bold. We shall make an expedition to the dying holy man and try to gain both his blessing and his bear.

March 15th, 1810 (March 3rd O.S.)

While travel in far northern latitudes in the cold seasons is never easy, it is much eased by the power of a wealthy nobleman. The Count had rightly judged that for Boris to woo his potential mate, the whole tribe of bears must be called into action, and it was a large party equipped with sleighs and horses and well stocked with provisions that took ship from Archangel.

The farther shore is sparsely inhabited. We landed at the small village of Tetrino, a few wooden houses around an onion-domed wooden church, where the Count has recruited a local man, Misha, to guide us to the Sami settlement.

March 20th, 1810 (March 8th O.S.)

Our company of bears now numbers eleven! It was a short journey to the Sami settlement. I was surprised to see conical tents like the *teepees* made by the natives of North America, but perhaps this is the easiest form of tent to make if you have a supply of straight branches to support it.

Here we were introduced to Turi, the *noaidi* or holy man of the local people, whose role is to mediate between the many deities of their polytheistic religion and the people. He was indeed very old and it was clear that his life was ebbing, but when he saw bears and humans in harmony, his wrinkled face brightened. He explained through Misha that the bear was wandering not far way, and that he would call her with his spiritual powers. She is called Beaivi, after the Sami sun goddess who is the mother of mankind. Sure enough she came, and Boris watched her eagerly as she approached.

We stood around as they sniffed each other, and it was clear that there was an instant bond between them – two bears brought up by men, far from their own kind. We knew that they were now mates, but Turi confirmed it for the humans by singing a long sacred song. The language was incomprehensible, but each line ended with a kind of refrain, *voia voia* or *nana nana*, and sometimes both. In its complexity it reminded me of the Orthodox wedding liturgy. Anyway, Boris and Beaivi are now married in the sight of Ipmil – the Samis' god who created the world – and bears and men. As for the couple, I have never seen happier bears.

We said our farewells to Turi – and may Ipmil look mercifully on him when he passes – and the Count left a present of money for the village. Then we returned to the ship, and I write this as we are sailing back to Archangel.

19.

March 29th, 1810 (March 17th O.S.).

We have good news brought by one of the Count's agents returning from St Petersburg. A suitable ship has been found and purchased, and is now on her long way around the Norwegian coast to Archangel. She is the Danish ship *Dronning Bengjerd*, named after the medieval Queen Berengaria, the Portuguese-born consort of the Danish King Valdemar II in the 13th century. I hope that the Portuguese name, though mangled by northern tongues, is a good omen for us after our military success in that country.

April 5th, 1810 (March 24th O.S.).

Our ship has arrived in Archangel harbour, and we have gone out to her to inspect the Count's new acquisition. The word 'ship' is perhaps too elegant to describe this dumpy little vessel of 325 tons displacement, whose lines recall a bathtub more than a majestic man of war. But there is no doubt that she is very strongly built, and will serve our purpose well enough,

The master of the ship on her voyage, Ilya Ulyanov, told us that she sails 'like a pig', rolling heavily, responding sluggishly to the helm, and sagging badly downwind. No matter: we are not buying a racing yacht.

To our surprise, she arrived fully armed with two 10-inch mortars and 12 guns of various sizes, and with a reasonable supply of powder, mortar bombs and cannonballs for all of them. We shall keep all these things on our voyage. The bombs may prove useful if we need to blast a passage through the ice.

April 7th, 1810 (March 26th O.S.).

The *Dronning Bengjerd* is now in dock, being strengthened for her voyage. Extra frames are being inserted at the fore end, and on the outside the copper sheathing at the bow (whose purpose is to resist the *Teredo* shipworm, which eats its way into the wood) is being removed to make way for an extra layer of oaken strakes. The forward edge of the bow will be armed with iron plates, protecting the hull from abrasion when butting through pack ice. The copper will not be replaced here, as it would only be torn off. Also, it has been observed that when copper and iron are placed close together in sea water the iron is quickly eaten away – something that might be explained by our friend Sir Humphry Davy, were he present.

We are also laying in supplies for what may prove a long voyage. I am concerned about the likelihood of scurvy among the sailors when we are to spend months living on ship's rations. It has certainly killed more sailors than the enemy's guns ever did. When I was at Cambridge I read James Lind's book *A Treatise of the Scurvy*, whose author describes how, having made experiments on groups of sailors, he discovered that eating fresh fruit, particularly lemons and oranges, protected them from the disease. That is not a luxury we can offer them in the frozen north.

However, Captain James Cook kept his sailors healthy on his long voyage by making them eat the smelly German fermented cabbage called *Sauerkraut*, and this is readily available so we have ordered a plentiful store of barrels. Cook found his men unwilling to eat the stuff and one can hardly blame them, but administering a dose before the rum ration should have the desired effect.

Another antiscorbutic method which has been proved effective is to eat freshly sprouted leaves. Even on a ship in the Arctic it is possible to germinate cress seeds on blankets moistened with fresh water, though it is hard to produce enough for a ship's crew. I have read that the Chinese did the same on long voyages with ginger plants, but we have no ginger root here and do not know how to grow it anyway.

We bears do not suffer from scurvy.

April 17ᵗʰ, 1810 (April 10ᵗʰ O.S.)

This is Easter Sunday in the Old Style calendar, though the vagaries of the system for determining the date of Easter decreed by the Council of Nicaea in A.D. 325 cause us in England to celebrate it on the following Sunday. We have attended all the services for the three days in the Count's chapel, and now people are greeting each other with joyful shouts of '*Khristos voskres*', 'Christ is risen.' We have had a grand feast of *kulich*, a kind of sweet bread; *paskha*, which literally means Easter but here refers to a dish made of cottage cheese, raisins and nuts; and of course eggs, dyed red by boiling them wrapped in onion skin.

We cannot continue to celebrate festivals twice. When Christ is risen, He is risen and, in the words of Dr Johnson, 'there's an end on 't.'

May 12ᵗʰ, 1810 (April 30ᵗʰ O.S.).

Work is finished on the ship, and our stores are being loaded. Thanks to the good Count, our expedition is provisioned for every eventuality. We shall be in known waters until we reach Novaya Zemlya, but the territory beyond that is largely unexplored, and we are carrying a store of the traditional gifts to secure the good will of any natives we may encounter: knives, mirrors and glass beads.

We also expect our voyage to be a slow one, and are setting out well in advance of the least annual extent of sea ice, which occurs in early autumn. We should be able to reach Novaya Zemlya without undue obstruction, and will then wait for the first opportunity to depart. It is better to be too early than too late. However, as Homer says, Ἀλλ' ἤτοι μὲν ταῦτα θεῶν ἐν γούνασι κεῖται, But truly these things rest on the knees of the gods.

Of the ship's original crew of thirty-two, twenty men including Master Ulyanov have declared themselves willing to take part in our voyage. The more faint-hearted will be able to find themselves berths on ships leaving Archangel for more southerly destinations, and we do not need such timid folk on what may prove an arduous expedition. We bears, Fred, Jem, Dolores and the indomitable Count will more than make up the deficiency. The Count is also bringing one manservant, Dmitri, to attend to his personal needs; he is a good enough fellow but we cannot know how well he will fare in the ice.

It is curious that our host, blessed with a considerable fortune and good looks and in the prime of life, has not seen fit to marry. Perhaps he is too set in his enthusiasm for exploration to trouble himself with affairs of the heart, or perhaps his tastes lie elsewhere. It is not for me to enquire.

May 14th, 1810 (May 2nd O.S.).

We are under way. Yesterday, which was a Sunday, we attended a service of blessing for our voyage, and may it stand us in good stead for the difficulties to come. Our spirits are high and we have good hopes of success but, to quote Homer again, Ἀλλ' οὐ Ζεὺς ἄνδρεσσι νοήματα πάντα τελευτᾷ, Yet Zeus does not fulfil all the designs of men.

As Ulyanov warned us, the ship is a fat wallowing tub, slow and unmanageable, and the strengthening work has no doubt made her worse. Even with a brisk wind she struggles to make six knots, and tacking into a headwind is a sad crawl. However, we are not in a hurry, and no doubt the stout hull will prove an advantage when we are in the ice.

Our polar bears have never been on a ship before, but are already enjoying climbing up the rigging. We are showing them the ropes – literally – and teaching them the skills and duties of sailors.

Dmitri is painfully seasick in little more than a flat calm.

May 17th, 1810 (May 5th O.S.).

We passed south of Kolguyev Island, a place that has not been fully surveyed. There is no reason to stop here, for it is uninhabited apart from temporary encampments of seal hunters.

That evening we had our first sight of an iceberg, a lofty and gleaming tower made all the more majestic by the gathering dusk. As every schoolboy knows, nine-tenths of an iceberg is under water, and the submerged portion extends for some way below the surface, so one must keep well clear of every one lest the ship be torn open by an unseen icy projection.

May 19th, 1810 (May 7th O.S.).

We have had our first encounter with pack ice, frozen out of the sea last winter and still only partly melted. So far it is not very thick, either in terms of the proportion of open water it occupies or as regards its depth from top to bottom, only a couple of feet in the main.

We keep a lookout constantly in the foretop, who scans the sea ahead for open passages running as nearly as possible in our desired direction, and thus we thread our way in a zigzag course. Occasionally it is necessary to butt our way through obstacles, and the hull resounds with heavy thumps and hideous screeches. At these times we are grateful for the Count's foresight in strengthening the hull and adding armour to the bow.

We can only make progress in the daytime when we can see clearly. During the nights, already very short in these northern latitudes, we moor the ship to a large ice floe. We have been out to explore one of these, but it was without the faintest trace of a living creature.

May 22nd, 1810 (May 10th O:S.).

We sighted Novaya Zemlya yesterday afternoon. Sailing up the west coast we encountered a Norwegian whaling ship, the *Hvalross*, which means 'walrus'. The Count, Ulyanov, Fred, Jem and myself went across in a boat to confer with the captain. When he had recovered from the shock of seeing a bear coming over the side we had a conversation in a mixture of bad Russian and worse German. He told us that the ice to the east is still thick, and we should wait for a while before penetrating it. He advised us to put in at an inlet a short way to the north, where there is a settlement of Pomor seal hunters.

The Pomors are Russians, principally from Novgorod, who have sailed around and inhabited this region for some centuries – the name *Pomor* means 'seagoers'. They form the bulk of the very small population of these islands, along with a handful of the native Samoyed people – and even they, with their skills at living in the northern waste, find this barren land unrewarding. Neverthelss, it is claimed by the Russian crown. Well, we bears claim our territories of a few square miles, and humans do the same on a grander and thoroughly pretentious scale. Here I see nothing but an icy wilderness that belongs to no one, though further examination may reveal more.

May 23rd, 1810 (May 11th O.S.).

We found the Pomor settlement in a sheltered bay, a small collection of shacks constructed from driftwood, whale bones, rough stones and sailcloth, and have moored our ship and gone ashore. The inhabitants were awed by the arrival of a Count and frankly shocked by the presence of bears. It seems that there is a running war between the settlers and the local polar bears – hardly surprising, as humans have invaded the bears' territory. Assured of their safety by the Count, beguiled by a hastily conducted dance, and seduced by gifts, they have accepted us as benign visitors; but things may be different elsewhere in this remote place.

May 25th, 1810 (May 13th O.S.).

Indeed my fears expressed in the last entry were well founded. The ever curious Count, eager to explore the natural history of an unknown land, mounted an expedition to the interior, taking with him Fred and Jem, and all the bears who were eager to feel snow under their paws again.

There is not much to see: an expanse of ice and rocks, and a few seabirds straggling in from the coast; but the bears' sensitive noses picked up traces of polar bears, whom we were eager to meet.

However, what we encountered was a dismal surprise. Our own two polar bears, Boris and Beaivi, were leading the way when we came across a party of hunters from another settlement. They were at once fired on, not accurately but Beaivi was grazed by a bullet. At once Boris, enraged by the wounding of his mate, rushed at them, and it was only by prompt intervention that we managed to stop him from tearing the whole party to shreds. Luckily we were able to hold down and disarm the five men without further

bloodshed. The Count gave them a severe lecture about their behaviour, which they pretended to heed, before returning their weapons and sending them on their way.

We may have to remain here for some time, and must maintain good relations with the local people, such as they are. Nevertheless, we have found ourselves in the midst of a bitter and endless conflict between men and polar bears. I wish it were otherwise, but the world is as we find it. As the old proverb has it, Δεὶ φέρειν τὰ τῶν θεῶν, We must bear the things that the gods send us.

20.

June 13th, 1810 (June 1st O.S.).

We have left Novaya Zemlya, to general relief, and are sailing down the west side of the island to resume our eastward course. No one enjoyed our sojourn in this Godforsaken place, least of all the bears who found themselves enemies of the inhabitants. Our supplies are replenished with what was on offer, so at least we have plenty of preserved seal meat (though even the polar bears think this is poor stuff) and extra gunpowder for exploding icy obstacles.

The temperature has risen since we arrived, and at present there is little ice to be seen. From what the inhabitants tell us, there will be more as we sail east. But we are well prepared, and have every hope that we can pass through it. As Sophocles wrote, Ἐλπὶς γὰρ ἡ βόσκουσα τοὺς πολλοὺς βροτῶν, For it is hope that maintains most mortals.

June 15th, 1810 (June 3rd O.S.).

Turning east through an unnamed strait, we find ourselves in uncharted waters, visited only by whaling ships.

The Dutch explorer Willem Barents penetrated a short way into this sea in 1597, but died among his scurvy-ridden crew who ran for home with their mission unaccomplished, less than a quarter of the way along the course they had planned to reach the eastern tip of the continent.

We will sail due east unless we are turned south by ice, and at some point we should find the coast of the mainland, after which we will keep close to it as far as we can. The farther we keep to the south, the less ice there should be. The ship's chronometer and a noon sighting tell us that we are now at 60° east, and a light westerly breeze carries us along in open water under a blue sky and the warming rays of the sun, low in the heavens in these northern latitudes despite the date being near to midsummer. Even this sluggish vessel seems willing to go, and all the crew are filled with hope of new discoveries. But one should remember the warning of Cleobulus, Εὐτυχῶν μὴ ἴσθι ὑπερήφανος, ἀπορήσας μὴ ταπεινοῦ, Be not elated by good fortune, nor downcast by adversity.

June 20ᵗʰ, 1810 (June 8ᵗʰ O.S.).

Yesterday we made landfall, on a coast running from north to south at 67° east by our reckoning – how quickly we notch up degrees in these Arctic latitudes! Thinking it might be merely an island, we sailed south, only to find that the coast curved and forced us back the way we came. So we have assumed that it is a peninsula and turned north again, hoping to sail around its northern extremity.

Pack ice often slows our progress. We encountered walruses on a floe, but they offered no guidance as to our best route.

June 22nd, 1810 (June 10th O.S.).

We continue to sail northwards, and are now at 72° north, the nearest to the Pole that we have ever been. Surely this promontory cannot continue for ever.

Poor seasick Dmitri was vomiting over the side when he leant too far and fell into the freezing sea, whose chill can kill a frail human in a few minutes. Fortunately Boris and Beaivi, who were in the rigging on that side of the ship, saw him go and immediately dived in as we hastily hove to and lowered a boat. Swimming as only polar bears can, they swiftly brought him back and carried him up a straining rope ladder – the size of polar bears is a real test of our cordage. We stripped off his clothes, wrapped him in blankets, put him next to the galley stove, and plied him with heavily sugared tea laced with spirits to help him recover from the shock. By the time he had stopped shivering he was laughing about his brush with Death. Euripides reminds us, Ἡδύ τοι σωθέντα μεμνῆσθαι πόνων, It is sweet to remember troubles when you are in safety.

June 24ᵗʰ, 1810 (June 12ᵗʰ O.S.).

At last we have come to the northernmost extremity of this obstructive peninsula, and are resuming our eastward course through a strait to the south of an island. On both sides the land is flat, barren and icy, offering no landmarks, and our only clues to our position on the globe are what our chronometer and sextant tell us. We have almost reached 71° east and, if a magic carpet were to bear us due south, we would find ourselves in western India. But we have no magic to aid us, and we are still far from a destination of which we know almost nothing.

Nevertheless, all the crew, bears and men, are in high spirits as we sail into the unknown. We have ample stocks of food and drink, and there is music and dancing. Dmitri is no longer sick after his involuntary salt water cure. It is remarkable how a shock can reform the mind.

June 30ᵗʰ, 1810 (June 18ᵗʰ O.S.).

We are in sight of the coast again. Its angle drives us ever northwards, and we are already at 75° north and the ice is thickening. We pass to the south of what seem to be scattered islands, though in these latitudes it is hard to distinguish between islands and icebergs.

July 1ˢᵗ, 1810 (June 19ᵗʰ O.S.).

Staying close to the shore has its disadvantages. The winds we have been encountering are light and variable, and there is little danger of being driven on to a lee shore and wrecked by a gale. But there is a constant risk of striking some projection in the shallow water, and that is what we have done.

The tide in these regions rises and falls only a few feet, owing to the obliquity of the tidal pull from the moon, and its timing is strangely irregular. Nevertheless, we are stranded on a mud bank in a falling tide, and must wait for it to rise again before we can contrive to get ourselves off it.

July 2ⁿᵈ, 1810 (June 20ᵗʰ O.S.).

We are free, though it took the combined power of bears and men rowing as hard as they could in three boats to drag us off the obstruction at the top of the tide. The strengthened hull of the ship is completely undamaged, and we proceed on our way. However, we find increasing difficulty in threading our way through the pack ice.

Dolores is now feeling as sick as Dmitri did, though with a different cause. Apparently this is a usual event in human pregnancy, which makes me ever more glad to be a bear and free of such foibles – I never felt better than when I was carrying dear Bruin. However, she makes light of her troubles, and they will pass.

July 13ᵗʰ, 1810 (July 1ˢᵗ O.S.).

We are now at 78° north and 104° west, and most likely in a place where no ship has yet penetrated. If a crow flew due south from here – as any sensible crow instantly would from this barren icy waste – it would eventually find itself in Singapore; and in my weaker moments I cannot help wishing that we were there too.

The ice is no longer an impediment to our progress: it is a barrier. Yesterday we proceeded a few miles by going on to a floe and blowing it apart with gunpowder, but today the ice ahead of us is so dense that I fear we may have to wait for further melting as summer progresses. But melt it will, and we must not be impatient. Our ship is strong, and we have supplies for many months.

July 15ᵗʰ, 1810 (July 3ʳᵈ O.S.).

Fast in ice, and free of the usual duties of the ship, we are free to disport ourselves as we please. The sailmaker has made us an excellent though strangely hairy football out of a seal's bladder covered with its skin. We have also tried cricket, with a ball of cork covered in leather and a bat hewn out by the carpenter, but this has not been a success as the ball bounces oddly on the ice and the Russians are baffled by the game's arcane rules.

However, everyone enjoys a quaint old English game called 'base-ball', which can best be compared to a circular game of cricket without wickets. The bowler stands in the middle and casts balls at the batsman, who may be anywhere in a ring of 'bases' marked around the perimeter and carries a rounded club like a larger version of a belaying pin. If the batsman strikes a ball with sufficient force to send the opposing fielders chasing it, he may run to the next base, or the one after that, and so on around the circle until the ball is brought back. If he does not reach a base in time, a ball thrown at the base will cause him to be run out, just as in cricket. It is all delightfully simple and easy to understand, and bears, Englishmen and Russians are all enjoying the game.

Needless to say, we bears have the upper hand in this sport, since we can both hurl and strike the ball with great force, and run like the wind. But by assigning equal numbers of bears and humans to each side we can make the game fair. I feel that if cricket had not somehow gained the ascendancy, base-ball might have come to be the sport of our nation. Maybe it will have greater success elsewhere.

July 25ᵗʰ, 1810 (July 13ᵗʰ O.S.).

The crew are beginning to fret in their icy prison, even the easygoing Fred. He was watching Jem polishing the compass binnacle, which did not need polishing but there was nothing else to do, and was quietly singing to himself 'Why are we waiting?' to the tune of *Adeste fideles*. 'Will yer stop droning that bloody dirge!' he snapped. Jem was taken aback and apologised, saying that he had no idea he was doing it. What a strange murky thing the human mind is, with its shallow and deep currents. Fred accepted his apology and the matter is closed, but it shows how everyone is on edge.

The Greeks and the Romans called the Arctic Sea the Sea of Cronos, the monstrous Titan who emasculated his father and devoured his children. Pliny called it *Mare Pigrum*, the idle sea, and others *Mare Concretum*, the clotted sea; while the Celts called it *Morimarusa*, which the Romans translated correctly as *Mare Mortuum*, the sea of the dead. All these names seem apt to us as we languish in its grip.

July 30ᵗʰ, 1810 (July 18ᵗʰ O.S.).

At last we are free! At dawn as usual, we sent a lookout to the main masthead, and he spotted clear water to the east. We have spent the rest of the day blasting a passage to it through the ice, firing mortar bombs to break the floes and give us a passage to the open sea. We have expended ten of the twenty-five bombs we had, but with good fortune we should not have to do this again.

Now we are under way, threading our course through loose floes with a lookout constantly up the foremast to advise us of obstacles. So far the path seems clear as we sail southeast to make landfall again and try to find the narrow strait discovered by Vitus Bering in 1728, which separates the eastern tip of Asia from the west coast of America. With the primitive

reckoning of his time, Bering could not give an accurate reading of the longitude of this passage, but we know that it lies at 65° north, well to the south of our present position, and at about 168° *west* – that is, we have to go so far to the east that it becomes west again.

But our hearts are high, and we are all confident that we shall complete our mission, and escape this frozen region to break out into the Pacific Ocean and admire the wonders of the gorgeous east.

21.

August 28th, 1810 (August 16th O.S.).

Finally we are through the strait between Asia and America. After our long sojourn in a region where the chart shows only pictures of sea monsters, we are again in a place that has been surveyed, however inaccurately.

It has been a long haul, but once we were free of the ice we encountered no substantial obstacles beyond a few floes that had to be avoided. As these became less frequent, we halted at one to hack off ice to replenish our water supply. This we put in a spare sail to melt, and we now have fresh water aplenty. Boris and Beaivi caught five seals, a welcome addition to our dwindling supplies of meat. The large store we have taken on board does not last long on a ship crewed by bears.

We are now within sight of the two small Diomede Islands that lie in the middle of the strait – and on a most significant day, because in the Old Style calendar this is the eighty-second anniversary of their first sighting by Vitus Bering in 1728. (Of course at this time England too was using the old calendar.) Like many islands, they are named after the saint on whose day they were discovered. St Diomedes was a Christian physician who died around A.D. 300 after arrest by the agents of the Emperor Diocletian. History does not recall the manner of his death, but having seen what the English agents of law and order do to the folk they arrest, I can hazard a guess. It is said that when the soldiers brought his severed head to the emperor, all who saw it were struck blind and did not recover their sight until the head was reunited with its body. He is revered as one of the Holy Unmercenaries – people who perform good acts without asking for payment – since he did not charge for his medical services.

For us too it is a day to celebrate: a successful voyage through the Northeast Passage. I believe that we are the first to complete this arduous course. As Ovid put it, *Nos fragili vastum ligno sulcavimus aequor*, We have ploughed the vast ocean in a fragile bark. I think it not immodest to claim that we could have not have done so without the aid of us eleven bears, whose strength greatly supplemented the power of the human crew to overcome the many obstacles in our path.

Perhaps, when ships driven by steam engines have come into their own, it may be possible to use this route for commerce. A convoy led by a powerful and well armoured vessel to break through the ice would have a good chance of success, at least in a warm summer when the ice melts adequately. But it is far from an easy voyage, and I think that for some years trading vessels will be taking the old long course around Europe and Africa into the Indian Ocean, a hazardous route but less arduous that the one we have followed.

Count Bagarov and Master Ulyanov are agreed that we should not try to retrace our route to return to Archangel. By the time we were halfway through, winter would have set in and the ice would be advancing. Therefore we shall sail south and west, through the fabled Indies, and who knows what we shall find?

September 10ᵗʰ, 1810 (August 29ᵗʰ O.S.).

Sailing south, we have sighted some islands of the Catherine Archipelago, a chain of islands stretching between Russia and the Russian territory of Alaska on the American side. Rocky and treeless, they appeared at first to be uninhabited, but we saw smoke rising from a small settlement. We anchored and sent a boat ashore, with the Count, Fred and Jem, Bruin and myself.

We found a party of natives hunting sea otters, which are valued for their pelts. One of them spoke some Russian and, once he had recovered from his surprise at encountering a mixed party of bears and men, and

had been gratified by the present of some steel knives, he told us that his people are called the Unangas. They scrape a living from the barren land which they supplement by selling otter pelts to the Russians, but in recent years the Russians have been cheating them by reducing the payment for these, and there has been violent conflict. (The Count wisely kept silent during this conversation. The natives do not know who we are, but assume that we are at least not Russians.)

We asked him whether there was a larger settlement where we could purchase supplies for our ship, and he told us that there was an island to the west called Atta, where there was a Russian town – but as he did so, he spat on the ground to show his contempt for the invaders.

Nevertheless we must head there, for after our long voyage we are running short of many of those essential things that keep a ship afloat – cordage, tar, gunpowder, salt meat and spirits – and must replenish them as far as we can from such remote outposts.

September 14th, 1810 (September 2nd O.S.).

We anchored in the harbour of Atta, the small town on the island of the same name. It is barely more than a village, but the trade in otter and seal pelts keeps it prosperous enough and we managed to restore our supplies to some extent. The good Count seems to have a limitless supply of Maria Theresia thalers, a currency recognised as genuine in the remotest parts of the world.

The local Russians call the native people Aleuts and despise them as savages, while they rely on them to supply the furs they deal in. It is plain that anger on both sides is still burning after the battles of twenty years ago.

We were glad to up anchor and sail away from this miserable place.

September 30ᵗʰ, 1810 (September 18ᵗʰ O.S.).

We have made good progress with a following wind driving our ambling vessel as fast as she will go down a chain of small islands flanking the east coast of the mainland, and are now arrived at the northernmost large island of Japan, which our chart names as Hokkaido. Knowing nothing of this mysterious kingdom, we put in at the first bay where there seemed to be a reasonable anchorage and signs of human habitation.

Here we were greeted not by anyone who met our expectations of what Japanese people would look like, but by a group of beetle-browed, heavily bearded men whose eyes suggested a European rather than an oriental heritage. They wore long garments decorated with bold geometric patterns. We did not know what to make of them, nor they of us – but the fact that our landing party included four bears provoked more than the usual attention, and we sensed a certain reverence in them.

The usual scrabble for mutually intelligible languages ensued. One of the people spoke a certain amount of Malay – evidently he had been a sailor in regions to the south where this is a *lingua franca* – and so did Misha, one of the Russian sailors who had also served thereabouts.

In this way we discovered that these people call themselves the Ainu, and they are the original inhabitants of the northern part of Japan and the islands we had just passed. The Japanese who have taken control of Hokkaido regard them as worthless savages and treat them with disdain, and have driven them into corners of the island.

We were invited to their village, where we were surprised to find that their womenfolk appeared to have luxuriant moustaches. On closer inspection, these were revealed to be black tattoos around the mouth, which are considered beautiful ornaments by these people.

We also discovered that they view bears as sacred – but, as so often with humans, this regard cuts both ways, for they also hunt bears and sacrifice them to their gods. As visitors in companionship with humans we are safe from persecution, but we do not feel at ease here. However, a performance of dances in the village left them mightily impressed, and all is harmonious for the time being.

I am concerned for Dolores, who must be approaching the time when she gives birth. She is hopping around as merrily as the rest of the crew, but I sense that her fortitude masks a most uncomfortable heaviness.

October 9th, 1810 (September 27th O.S.).

We had been pursuing our southwesterly course with a fair wind for several days, but this afternoon the wind changed rapidly, at first to easterly and then backing to the south, while black clouds were evident ahead. It was clear that a storm was approaching. Knowing nothing of these latitudes or longitudes, we thought it wise to prepare for the worst eventuality.

Master Ulyanov ordered us to strike all sails except main and fore topsails, a task that took some time as the wind freshened. We also brought out a storm trysail from the locker. This is a small fore-and-aft sail which is attached to the mainmast and used to keep a ship under way when the wind is so strong that no other sail can stand.

We have battened down the hatches – that is, we have laid timbers across them and lashed these to the cleats on the deck – tied down the boats, rigged lifelines along the deck, and made whatever other preparations we can. In Virgil's words, *Quo fata trahunt, retrahuntque, sequamur*, Let us go wherever the fates drive us or drive us back. I will now stop writing and wrap this journal securely in oilcloth.

October 10th, 1810 (September 28th, O.S.).

What a night it has been! As evening approached the wind, already strong, increased to a gale, and then beyond a gale to unimaginable force. Waves towered mast-high, and we laboured up toward the crest, paused for a moment in the shrieking, foaming confusion at the summit, and slid back into the valley on the other side. The ship rolled until sometimes she was almost on her beam ends, but the sturdy vessel always dragged herself upright.

We had reefed the sails as far as they would go, and soon had to take them in entirely and rely on the single storm trysail to give us as much way as we needed to steer the ship and keep her head into the wind. We were all fearful that even this tiny scrap of canvas would carry away and leave us wallowing and foundering in the gigantic waves.

As the sun set invisibly behind the stormclouds, Angelina told me that I was needed below. It took only a glance and a sniff at Dolores to know that she was in labour, perhaps induced by the battering that we were all receiving in the wildly rolling vessel. The five female bears,

Angelina, Mary, Emily, Beaivi and myself, rallied to assist her at this most difficult of times in the most hazardous of situations. We lashed her securely to a cot while we held on to any support we could find as the cabin tilted crazily one way and the other.

I had not witnessed a human birth before, and was astonished at how arduous it was, and how painful for the mother. The human frame seems so ill adapted for childbirth that it is a wonder that the human race has contrived to multiply. Dolores is as courageous as any warrior, but even she could not restrain her shrieks as the birth pangs racked her, and I was reminded of the meaning of her name. However, as Aeschylus said, Οἱ δὴ στεναγμοὶ τῶν πόνων κουφίσματα, Lamentations are a sure relief of dolours.

Meanwhile, the raging storm suddenly subsided, and we found ourselves in a windless calm. Master Ulyanov came below and shyly poked his head around the corner, unwilling to intrude on this private scene. He said only, 'Do not be deceived. We are in the eye of a circular storm. Soon it will blow again, as hard as before.' Then he vanished.

It was during these few minutes of welcome relief that Dolores was delivered of a healthy baby boy. I knew enough to hold the infant upside down to clear his lungs and pat him gently on the back until he started crying, then I put him into the arms of his pale, bloody but triumphant mother. It was a moment of joy – but all too brief, as the wind was getting up again and we were needed on deck. I waited for just long enough to bite through the umbilical cord, then followed the other bears up.

As the storm resumed its raging, this time from the west, we were relieved to see that so far our ship had weathered the hurricane in reasonable order – or I should say the typhoon, as such events are termed in the Pacific, that ill named and unruly ocean. All the masts, yards and rigging were intact, but one of the three boats had been torn from its lashings and had gone overboard. The storm trysail was tattered but holding. We prepared for another onslaught – and it came, even harder than before.

When folk are in peril niceties may be dispensed with, but not essentials. In case we should perish in the renewed tempest, it was necessary for the boy to be christened, and Master Ulyanov exercised his privilege to perform the baptism according to what he could remember of the Orthodox rite. At my suggestion we named him Aeolus for the god of the winds, and his second name was Jeremy after his father. I am sure that a just God will forgive us any deficiencies in the ritual.

I write this in the small hours of the morning, as the typhoon is subsiding into no more than an ordinary rough sea, which seems like a flat calm after what we have endured. We have weathered the storm with no further damage, and have even managed to hoist topsails again and continue on our way.

Mother and baby are well. There is further good news: Dmitri was not seasick at all during the storm, and is at last managing to pull his weight with the rest of the crew.

22.

We sail on, occupied by many small repairs necessary after the storm. Damaged blocks have to be replaced, and lashings that have worked loose need remaking. Yet all in all our sturdy old tub has stood up well to its ordeal.

So has Dolores, who is now up and walking painfully about on the heaving deck. I now understand why Euripides' Medea says:

Λέγουσι δ' ἡμᾶς ὡς ἀκίνδυνον βίον
ζῶμεν κατ' οἴκους, οἱ δὲ μάρνανται δορί,
κακῶς φρονοῦντες· ὡς τρὶς ἂν παρ' ἀσπίδα
στῆναι θέλοιμ' ἂν μᾶλλον ἢ τεκεῖν ἅπαξ.

Men say we live a carefree life at home
Out of harm's way, while they fight with the spear.
How wrong! – for I would rather stand three times
In battle with my shield, than once give birth.

But little Aeolus is a delight, and all the female bears are clamouring for a chance to hold him.

We are headed for Canton in China, where there are large shipyards and we can equip ourselves for the voyage home. There are also a fair number of Jews, which will allow Count Bagarov to avail himself of their unique and valuable service. If you possess a fair fortune and a good reputation you may borrow money from any Jewish man of business in the farthest corner of the world, and pay the money back later, with a not unreasonable commission, to another Jew in an equally remote location such as Archangel, and somehow the transaction will be communicated across the world, though it may travel at the pace of an ambling horse. The system depends on the honour of all parties involved, which may not be inviolate; but despite the occasional abuse it has stood for many years and is an indispensable boon to voyagers such as ourselves.

October 20th, 1810.

We are in Canton, whose sheltered harbour is reached by sailing up the broad estuary of the Pearl River. Far as it is from home, I feel that we are back in the familiar world, and here it is unequivocally October the 20th and from now on I shall abandon the Old Style dates, as the crew and even the Count have been obliged to do. They can lose their twelve days' difference when they are safely back in Russia.

This is a port city, not unlike others of its kind such as Bristol, except that it is inhabited by Chinese. Folk are much the same the world over, and perhaps the main difference is that the food is much better. The streets are full of little stalls where the most delicious little things are dispensed for a few pence, and we bears have been indulging ourselves

mightily. In a city where foreign visitors abound language may be dispensed with, and signs will secure us everything we need – perhaps at an inflated price for outsiders, but still a bargain. I have never felt less hampered by my lack of human speech.

The sailors too have been availing themselves of the local delights. Their principal goal has been what are euphemistically named 'flower boats', which are – to put it indelicately – floating bordellos. Those in Canton itself are reserved for the Chinese, but only a short distance to the east in Whampoa there are similar boats which offer the same services in a less delicate form for foreigners. Should anyone contract an infection, a Chinese barber will cure it with oriental herbs with an ease and speed unthinkable in England, where they poison you with mercury until you are half dead in the hope that the illness will be three quarters killed, but it always returns.

Our good ship the *Dronning Bengjerd* too is in need of what services the port can provide. Her seams have been strained by her being first trapped in ice and then battered by a storm, and she is leaking sadly – latterly we have had to spend a good two hours a day pumping her out. While she is in dock being recaulked, we shall have the extra layer of wooden armour removed from the bow, as it has been much mangled by butting through the ice and in these waters is now no more than impediment to sailing. We have carried the removed copper sheathing with us in the ballast, and this shall be replaced to serve its purpose in excluding the shipworm that bores into the hull.

To negotiate this work we have enlisted the services of a Chinese agent named Rongwei, who speaks both Russian and English with some fluency.

He has secured us a contract at a fraction of the price we would pay in a western dockyard, and the task is being carried forward with remarkable speed. Rongwei said that, should we wish to abandon our cumbersome European ship and purchase a serviceable Chinese junk, he could arrange for one of any desired size to be constructed for us in a few weeks.

To drive home his point, he took us on a little voyage down the estuary in a junk, and we were all surprised at how handy the ungainly vessel was, and how well its peculiar sails made of matting strengthened by bamboo slats functioned even when sailing close to the wind. The Count praised the junk but gracefully declined the offer, saying that it was best to stick to what he was used to. Rongwei took this in good part, and in fact I think his real object had been to demonstrate to us the superiority of his nation over a band of foreign barbarians, however good their money.

November 1st, 1810.

This morning we brought our ship out of the dock, fully repaired and watertight and as good as ever she was. Our provisions are fully restocked, and we are ready to set a course for the East Indies. Men and bears have reported for duty – but where is Bruin? No one has seen him since yesterday afternoon. My mother's heart is racked with anxiety. We have been quartering the city in an effort to pick up his scent, without result so far. The search continues into the night, and I write this in haste before going out again.

November 2nd, 1810.

After an interminable night, at dawn Emily came galloping down to the quayside. Her sensitive nose had detected Bruin in a house on the northern outskirts of the city. She reported that it was surrounded by a walled courtyard and difficult of access. As the other bears straggled in to report, the Count, Fred, Jem and myself were drawing up a plan.

We agreed that, in a foreign city, we could have no recourse to the authorities who would take the part of the residents, however heinous

their actions. There was no alternative to a direct assault on the building, after which we would have to leave hastily to escape the consequences.

We enlisted the aid of Rongwei to hire two carts drawn by mules. Though he was aware of our plan to assault the people of his city, he was perfectly willing to aid us if well paid, for which he earned our heartfelt thanks. He explained that Bruin had probably been taken so that he could be killed and his organs used in preparing Chinese medicine – at which my heart froze, and from that moment on I could think of nothing except the coming attack.

Looking back more calmly on this moment, I can see that Chinese medicine, so beneficial in its use of herbs to cure sailors of a dose of the clap, has a superstitious and malignant side where useless nostrums cruelly obtained are sold at high prices in a vain attempt to shore up the fading virility of old men who should long ago have laid their lusts to rest.

On one of the carts we placed one of our two three-pounder deck cannon, a cumbersome thing but easily lifted by a couple of bears. The other was loaded with powder and ball for this weapon, with all the ship's axes kept for cutting away fallen rigging, and several large sledgehammers. Those of us who had them from the Spanish war carried our sabres in sheaths on shoulder straps. The Count, Fred and Jem, and a selected party of a dozen sailors, were armed with muskets, pistols, cutlasses and daggers. Thus accoutred, we set out through the streets in a fearsome procession that made bystanders creep into the shadows.

At the house, there was no doubt that Emily's acute senses had led us to the right place. We could all scent Bruin, and that he was in some distress. Yet we dared not call to him, for we needed the element of surprise on our side.

The house was behind a blank wall with a heavy gate. We set down our cannon, loaded and primed it, and trained it on the lock. One well-aimed ball smashed it to atoms, and before the smoke had cleared we were through and charging into the house, roaring with bloody fury. There was an answering call from the upper storey.

In a moment we were in the house. Most of the people fled for their lives, but the few who tried to resist were dealt with mercilessly. If a person's head has been torn from his shoulders, he can hardly complain to the authorities about his treatment.

Moments later we were at the top of the house smashing open the door of the room where Bruin was confined. He was in chains but – O! how my heart surged in relief – completely uninjured. A few axe blows and he was free. We descended the stairs like a thunderbolt and milled out into the courtyard.

A moment to heave the cannon back on to the cart – you never know when you might need to blow something to pieces – and we were off, leaving behind us a scene of devastation from which it would take a while for the survivors to stagger out and raise the alarm. We surged down the hill and made for the harbour as fast as the mules could canter when pursued by bears.

Master Ulyanov had brought the ship right up to the quayside, so there was no call for boats. He had also rigged a hoist for the heavier items. We swung the cannon aboard, followed by the unused ammunition and arms in a sling, then swarmed up the gangplank. It was the work of a few minutes to set sail, and then we were heading briskly down the Pearl River estuary, far ahead of any possible pursuit.

Bruin said that he had been at a market stall buying food when an unknown man had offered him one of his favourite titbits, a steamed bun filled with roasted pork. He could recall no more until he had woken up chained and confined. Evidently the treat had been infused with some soporific drug, of which no doubt the ingenious Chinese have an ample store.

I did not tell him of the fate he had escaped. My dear Bruin has endured a dreadful experience and I will not augment it with tales of horror. I enjoined bears and men to silence on this dismal subject.

November 4ᵗʰ, 1810.

We are bowling along on a south-south-easterly course with a brisk following breeze, bound for our next landfall in Batavia in the Dutch East Indies, where we hope for a more hospitable welcome. Yet let us not forget Juvenal's warning:

> *Omnibus in terris, quae sunt a Gadibus usque*
> *Auroram et Gangen, pauci dinoscere possunt*
> *Vera bona atque illis multum diversa, remota*
> *Erroris nebula.*

> In all the lands from Cádiz to the east
> And the far Ganges, very few are able
> To tell true good from many different things
> Or lift the cloud of error.

At least the Chinese shipyard has done fine work on the *Dronning Bengjerd*. The removal of the armour at the bow has made the ship a little swifter and more easy to handle, though it has not reduced her ponderous rolling in all but the lightest seas – but we are so accustomed to this that we barely notice it.

Dolores and little Aeolus continue to prosper, and are idolised by the crew, men and bears alike. Though it is said that it is unlucky to have a woman aboard, to have a birth is considered the height of good fortune. Let us hope that these simple beliefs are justified.

23.

November 15ᵗʰ, 1810.

We have just crossed the Equator. Only one sailor on board, Misha, has been in the southern hemisphere before. He told us that it is customary for those who 'cross the line' for the first time to be subjected to a ceremony of humiliation in which members of the crew dress up as Neptune and his acolytes and perform various degrading acts upon them. From the expressions of the watching sailors and bears he inferred that this was not a welcome suggestion, and he did not press the matter. Instead, Master Ulyanov held a short service on deck in which he asked for God's blessing on our voyage south.

Boris and Beaivi, our two polar bears, have been increasingly feeling the heat of the tropics and need to cool themselves in the ocean, though even that is lukewarm in these climes. We have rigged a stout rope ladder at the stern of the ship, so that they can dive off the bow and swim for a few moments before climbing back up to the deck. They are such strong swimmers, and our ship is so leisurely in her progress, that there is no danger of them being left behind.

November 19ᵗʰ, 1810.

We are now at anchor in the harbour of Batavia, and have come ashore to explore the city. It is a tidy place with public buildings in the Dutch style,

tempered with a few oriental domes. Much work is in progress, as the old town built by the natives has been levelled and is being reconstructed in a manner more congenial to the European taste.

The island of Java on which the city stands, and adjacent islands of the Malay archipelago, were administered by the Dutch East India Company until twelve years ago, when the government of the Netherlands assumed power. However, since 1806 that government has been no more than a puppet of the French invaders under the Corsican tyrant's brother Louis Napoleon. In the summer of this year the almighty Emperor, finding that his brother was supporting Dutch interests rather than French ones, deposed him and assumed direct rule of the Netherlands. There is now a danger that these islands will become no more than a French colony.

It was no surprise, therefore, to hear that an English visitor was in the same place as ourselves. Misha, our Malay speaker, relayed this rumour to the Count, and we set off to discover its truth. And indeed we found English sailors, who told us that the visitor was named Stamford Raffles, and that he was a secretary of Lord Minto, the Governor General of India, and had been posted to Penang on the Malay peninsula to the north. Our experience of the British administration of their possessions told us that the apparently humble title of 'secretary' is awarded only to senior officials, and we resolved to seek him out.

November 20th, 1810.

How different this city is from Canton! There, life was conducted at a headlong pace, and all was bustle and noise. Here the inhabitants are of grave and gentle demeanour. Even the children are quiet and obedient. We found their character a little melancholy, and wondered whether it was due to a sad submission to rule by Europeans, or simply part of their nature.

However, my musings on the subject were soon interrupted by a distant commotion. The shouting grew, and it was apparent that some disturbance was heading our way. So it proved when a man burst into view in the broad street, screaming and slashing with a large curved knife resembling a cutlass. Bystanders cowered in the shadows as he advanced.

All eleven of us bears were present, with the Count, Fred, Jem, Dolores and Misha, and we confronted him in a formidable phalanx. But the man, clearly carried away with madness, was in no way deterred and rushed at us roaring and waving his knife.

We fell back as we had to, but an unspoken plan was taking shape. Bruin, Peter and William seized large pieces of bamboo lying at the roadside and advanced on the man, using their clubs to parry his thrusts. While he was thus distracted little Henry, the most nimble and stealthy

of the bears, slunk around the edge of the fight and crept up on him from behind.

It was over in a moment. Henry hooked a foot round the man's ankle and gave him a heavy blow between the shoulder blades, throwing him forward to grovel on his face in the dust, while his weapon went clattering away for us to retrieve it. Then Henry sat on him. He is only half grown but already twice as heavy as a man, so that concluded the fight.

The man was unconscious, either because he had hit his head in falling or because the shock of defeat had caused him to faint. After a few minutes he came to his senses. We were holding him firmly to rein in any further madness, but there was no need. He awoke blinking mildly at being surrounded by bears and foreigners, but there was no more fight in him. When questioned by Misha, he seemed to have no memory of what he had done.

The behaviour of the bystanders was also baffling. You might have expected them to be full of indignation and anger against a man who had run violently among them threatening to maim or kill all in his path. But they seemed to harbour no resentment, and even perhaps to be pleased that he had recovered from his frenzy.

Misha spoke to them and relayed their remarks to us. They explained that the man's madness was not an uncommon event among them, and called it *amok* or *gelap mata*, the latter term meaning 'the dark eye'. It was, they said, caused by demonic possession by a tiger spirit called *Hantu Belian*. Usually the possessed person – almost always a man – is killed or kills himself during his madness, but if he recovers he is not blamed for his acts, caused as they are by an external agency.

In the words attributed by Rabelais to Avicenna, *Maniae infinitae sunt species*, There are innumerable kinds of madness. I do not believe in tiger demons, and am inclined to attribute these outbreaks to the strain caused by the otherwise admirable control of self exhibited by the local population. When a man has, for any reason, a bitter grievance which he dare not show for fear of censure by his fellows, it may gnaw on his reason until it breaks and he runs *amok*.

November 22ⁿᵈ, 1810.

We did not need to seek out Stamford Raffles. Word travels swiftly in a small city, and the tale of a man running *amok* and saved by a party of bears was instantly the talk of the bazaar. He sent a servant to find our ship, with an invitation to visit him at his residence in the administrative quarter.

There we repaired, and were sumptuously entertained. Mr Raffles had sagely provided not merely a collation of local delicacies for his

human guests, but an ample sufficiency of raw meat of various kinds for the visiting bears, which we consumed with gusto and washed down with copious drafts of palm toddy, a refreshing beverage though no match for good English ale.

It was therefore in a benevolent mood that we bears sat in a half circle around Mr Raffles as he spoke with Count Bagarov, Fred, Jem and Dolores – and little Aeolus, in Dolores' arms. It is a tribute to his skill as a diplomatist that when the impeccably attired Count Bagarov greeted him with a shout of 'Wotcher, ole cock, 'ow's it 'angin'?' his eyebrows only rose for a fraction of a second.

Our host was suitably impressed by our feat in navigating the hitherto impassable North-East Passage, but his main concern was for the Dutch possessions in the archipelago, and what would become of them now that the puppet emperor Joseph Bonaparte had been cast aside. He was most interested in our experiences of the French occupation of Spain and Portugal, which Fred and Jem related to him with the full weight of

those who had been in the heart of the action. Fred's most important assertion was that it is impossible for an occupying army to gain full control of a country against the wishes of its people, which will prevail in the end against any foreign force.

However, Fred gracefully admitted that he might have been too close to the battle to take the long view, and deferred to my view as one who had absorbed the wisdom of the ancient historians. Mr Raffles, diplomatically concealing his surprise at being advised by a bear, therefore asked me for my opinion.

Taking up my slate and pencil, I wrote: *History has shown us that when power lapses in any region, another power will at once rush in and seize control of it. Never was this shown more clearly than in the fall of the western Roman Empire, whose final weakness led to its becoming a series of Gothic kingdoms. Here in the Indies, the collapse of the Dutch East India Company has led to the territory being administered by the Dutch government – as will surely happen in time to the lands administered by the English East India Company.*

As I wrote the last sentence, Mr Raffles could not restrain a grimace. I wiped the slate clean with a damp sponge and continued: *Power has now failed again in this region. With the fall of the petty emperor Joseph, there is now a vacuum that will certainly be filled by one of the nations of Europe.*

There can be no doubt that the French will be eager to rush in as soon as they can assemble a naval expedition, but this is impeded both by their distance from the scene and by British control of the seas. On the other hand, British forces (or rather, those of the Company) are available at a few days' notice. I would advise you to urge them to seize control and exclude our enemies the French.

Pausing to wipe the slate again, I wrote: *However, it would be a mistake to oust the Dutch in their hour of weakness, as we have a common enemy in the French. The territories should be taken with the publicly declared aim of restoring them to the Netherlands as soon as we have driven the French out of their homeland, an event which will inevitably ensue in a few years' time. Thus the English will continue to dominate their part of this region and the Dutch theirs, in reasonable rivalry. We do not wish to seize an over-extended empire that we cannot hold, as befell Alexander the Great and many other conquerors.*

I could see that Mr Raffles was impressed by my words, emerging somewhat Delphically from a squeaky slate – but I have always endeavoured to give advice in plain language, unlike that intoxicated and ambiguous oracle. There is some risk in such boldness: as Boethius is said to have remarked, *Si tacuisses, philosophus manisses*, If you had kept quiet, you would still be regarded as a philosopher. But I am a bear, and an an honest one, and I shall leave philosophy to others.

He replied. 'Thank you, Daisy, for your considered opinion. I am visiting Batavia for only a few days on my way to confer with my masters in India, and you have done much to make up my mind as to the advice I shall offer them. Whether they will take it remains to be seen; but I have found that the Company is always quick to seize an advantage, far quicker indeed than the cumbersome apparatus of governments. Whatever transpires, let us hope that we can keep the French out of this region.'

Mr Raffles also offered us some private advice: 'The trade in spices from the East Indies continues to be jealously guarded by the European powers that dominate the region. Here, however, power is in abeyance for the moment. What better time to load your ship with the riches of Nature, which may be sold for a thumping profit on your return?'

Count Bagarov, blessed as he is with the easy wealth of a landowner, is not averse to increasing it, and I could see him mentally calculating how much money he could borrow from the Jews of Batavia to purchase a lucrative cargo.

We bade Mr Raffles a cordial farewell as he made his preparations to depart. We too shall be gone soon, but there is still time for consultation. Later in the day and back at the port, Master Ulyanov and the captain of the naval vessel transporting Mr Raffles conferred, with the Count as interpreter, to determine our future course. The quickest way home for us is to follow the trade winds south-west into the open Indian Ocean, which will take us easily around the Cape of Good Hope and into the Atlantic. But it is a very long navigation of a desolate and unfrequented tract full of unknown dangers. On the other hand, to take a northward course closer to the land exposes us to other dangers, not least the negotiation of the east coast of Africa, where steady east winds drive ships on to a lee shore to join the throng of wrecks that litter the strand.

In the end it was the Count who decided the matter for us. He had, he said, read the tale of the Three Princes of Serendip as a boy, and had always longed to visit the happy island of Ceylon where these events are said to have occurred. Well, we have ventured east on his whim, and who will gainsay him wherever he wishes to go? I would like to see the place myself.

24.

December 1st, 1810.

We have crossed the Equator again, in the opposite direction. Our polar bears Boris and Beaivi must be the first of their kind to have ventured into the Southern Hemisphere, if only for a few days, but they miss the comforting coolness of the northern snows. Never mind, we are on our way home.

December 11th, 1810.

We are in Colombo, the principal city of Ceylon, situated a little way up the west coast so that we had to sail around the shore to reach it. Facing the mainland of India, the city is a stronghold of the East India Company. It is of the kind that we have learnt to expect in these parts, with a central administrative district built in a more or less European manner, which quickly fades into the native style as you leave the centre.

Knowing nothing of the local tongue, we engaged the services of a guide, Asiri, who spoke reasonable English. From him we learned that the Company controls a substantial portion of the coastline while the interior remains under the rule of the King of Kandy, Sri Vikrama Rajasinha. I suspect that his sway will not last more than a few years as the Company encroaches on his territory. Well, better their reasonably benevolent rule than the ramshackle tyranny of the French.

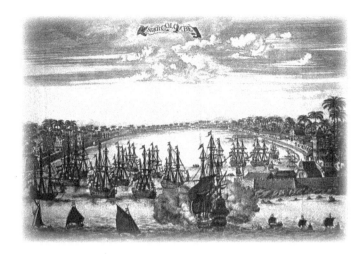

I was intrigued to find that the words in the local Sinhalese language for the first new numbers are *eka, deka, tuna, hatara, paha, haya, hata*. We are back in our own world again: compare the Greek words εἷς, δύο, τρεῖς, τέσσαρα, πέντε, ἕξ, ἑπτά. These people may be the most easterly outposts of the descendants of the ancient forerunners of both Europeans and the western Asiatic races. Such an idea was first expressed by Sir William Jones a few years ago, inspired by his studies of Greek, Latin and Sanskrit, but it is a surprise to find it supported in such a far-flung location.

Most of the population follow the religion of Buddha, which seems to keep them honest and respectable though I have my doubts about the moral value of its pursuit of spiritual perfection. In the words of our Lord as reported by St Mark, Ὃς γὰρ ἂν θέλη τὴν ψυχὴν αὐτοῦ σῶσαι, ἀπολέσει αὐτήν – which our English Bible translates as 'For whosoever will save his life shall lose it', but the word ψυχή might better be translated as 'soul'. Better to forget oneself and care for others.

These thoughts aside, they are a handsome and agreeable people, and relations between them and the Company men remain harmonious. Asiri says that the King is ill disposed to the settlers, as is only reasonable since they are gnawing at the edges of his kingdom. There has already been armed conflict between the two parties, and the city of Kandy, at the centre of the island, has been briefly occupied by a British military expedition. The King himself is said to be in the hands of a corrupt cabal of advisers whose only intention is to gain advantage from the present situation.

December 14th, 1810.

The island is an important producer of cinnamon. Count Bagarov is now alert to the possibility of financial profit from an expedition that he launched as a voyage of exploration, but I think that he is finding that even his considerable wealth is strained by the support of a ship constantly requiring repairs and stores, not to mention a hungry crew of bears and men. He is therefore purchasing a good stock of this spice.

The preparation of cinnamon is curious. The spice consists of the inner bark of a tree, which is stripped off and rolled into cylinders the size of a woman's little finger before being dried. These cylinders are bound together into a larger one, an operation requiring both strength and skill. The result is a bundle resembling a drum, which can conveniently be stowed in a barrel for shipment abroad.

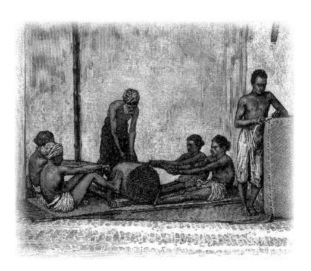

The *Dronning Bengjerd*, already redolent of nutmeg, cloves and cardamom, now smells overpoweringly of cinnamon. Seldom has there been a more fragrant ship. One scarcely notices the underlying reek of her occupants and their daily activities.

The food that we sample from stalls in the city is usually flavoured with the chilli fruit, a small red pod which gives it a taste that is often searingly fiery. Curiously, the plant is of central American origin and has only spread to these parts in recent years. At first we found the flavour daunting, but the palate soon adapts to its tickle and we now find food without chillies a little insipid. The Count has also bought a good store of dried chilli pods to take back to Russia, though he professes himself uncertain as to whether the people will take to it. In my view it might be more successful in England, much of whose staple food is so tasteless that the inhabitants feel the need to enliven it with pungent condiments made of mustard, pepper, ginger, anchovies and other strong-flavoured ingredients. When I think of the dismal fare I have consumed in English inns, it seems to me that an establishment offering the vividly flavoured dishes of Asia would be a roaring success.

December 16th, 1810.

I am astonished to say that we have encountered some more dancing bears, something hardly to be expected in an island so far from their natural haunts. Having sufficiently sampled the delights of Colombo – and, it has to be said, its noise and stink –
we were engaged in a ramble in the surrounding countryside.

We had stopped to admire a *dagoba* – a large stone structure resembling a bell that serves as a shrine for a relic of a Buddhist saint – when we heard the beating of a small drum and the snarl of a shawm. The sound came from a nearby village, to which we

hurried to find the cause of the celebration. Here we found two men gaily capering with two tiny bears scarcely taller, when standing on their hind legs, than the men themselves. Not wishing to cause a diversion, we watched the performance from a distance, but judged it an adroit one. We also noticed that the bears were not chained and seemed to be dancing willingly with their human companions, a sight that gladdened our hearts.

When the dance was finished and the men were passing round baskets for contributions from the spectators, we introduced ourselves to the amazement of all present. We learned through the translation of Asiri that bears and men alike came from the mountainous north of India, and had wandered around the vast peninsula and the isle of Ceylon much as I had travelled with Fred in our performing days. The bears were a couple named Rajah and Rani – 'king' and 'queen' in the Hindustani language – and the two men were called Sasthi and Amul.

They were awed by the size of the bears in our party, especially the two polar bears who were at least twice as tall as the royal couple.

We had, of course, told them that we were skilled in the dance, and a performance was requested. Luckily Jem always has his flute in his pocket, and we performed before them and the villagers in a style that astounded them. Our rendition of the Russian *gopak* left all speechless.

I wish I could have joined in that dance, but sadly I must admit that such feats are now beyond me. When I was in the library at Trinity in a gentle time that seems an age ago, I found in a dusty box a tattered ancient manuscript believed to be a late poem by Sappho, no longer a lusty young lass but an ageing woman recalling her youth. It contained the lines

> Βάρυς δὲ μ᾽ ὁ θῦμος πεπόηται, γόνα δ᾽ οὐ φέροισι,
> τὰ δὴ πότα λαίψηρ᾽ ἔον ὄρχησθ᾽ ἴσα νεβρίοισι.

My heart is heavy in my breast,
My knees are stiff and sore.
Once I could dance like a young fawn;
Such times will come no more.

Now more than ever I feel her regret. But I hasten to add that the apparent rhyme in the two lines of the original Greek is merely an accident. Rhyme had not been invented in Sappho's time, and the coincidence of endings would have passed unnoticed or actually have been condemned. When no less a person than Cicero wrote the pentameter line *O fortunatam natam, me consule Romam* – 'O fortunate Rome, born when I was consul' – Juvenal ridiculed it for its cacophony as much as its presumption.

We forbore to solicit contributions: the villagers had already given what they could to support their Indian visitors. While we were conversing amicably, if slowly, through the medium of Asiri, we heard strange cries and the noise of a commotion from the other side of the village, and all hastened to find the cause of the disturbance. And it was a considerable one, for an elephant employed by one of the villagers to carry felled trees had fallen into a steep-sided drainage ditch and, although uninjured, could not get out. He was trumpeting piteously, the sound that had we we had heard from a distance.

Rescue was a task that could clearly be accomplished only by a party of bears. But when we looked over the edge of the ditch, the poor creature was struck with panic and redoubled his cries. The owner told us that his elephant was particularly partial to a vegetable resembling kale, of which he had a stock. I took some under my arm and, at a reassuring distance from the elephant, climbed down the bank, and slowly and confidingly approached him, holding out my offering. To my relief, he accepted it.

It was time now for all the bears – and there were now a dozen of us! – to make our peace with the elephant and engage ourselves in the considerable task of raising him from the ditch. When he had recovered sufficiently from our approach and seen that we offered no threat, we conducted him to a part of the ditch where the sides sloped at a shallower angle. We had no proper way of communicating with this exotic beast, but for the time being gestures sufficed. Then we bundled him around to face up the steep slope, arranged ourselves around his massive grey hindquarters, and pushed with all our might.

As the elephant struggled up the first few feet of the slope we stood at the bottom of the ditch and had no difficulty in propelling him. Yet we had to raise him a good twenty feet, and the farther we went the less foothold we had. The huge Boris and Beaivi remained at the bottom, supporting us while we dug our feet into the ground and heaved two tons of elephant aloft. And we succeeded: at last the creature clambered up the last few feet of the incline and stood blinking while his owner embraced him and the villagers cheered.

The elephant is called Ranga, and his human Gihan. Overwhelmingly effusive congratulations were offered by all, and there were calls for a feast to celebrate the occasion. We were happy to join with them, but realised that the slim resources of a village would be entirely dispersed by accommodating the vast appetites of a party of bears, something that has strained even the ample resources of the Count on our voyage. Accordingly, he, Fred and Jem went off to the local market to purchase what food and drink they could find, while we bears repaired to the nearby river with Asiri to catch as many fish as possible.

Aided by the local knowledge of Asiri and the skilled paws of Boris and Beaivi, in a couple of hours we had a good haul, and returned to the village to find preparations well under way. And what a night we had! All difficulties with language vanished in the joy of the moment.

Replete with fish and rice, and animated with a local spirit distilled from coconut juice and called *arak*, we danced with Ranga the elephant far into the night, and finally collapsed on the warm ground in a happy heap.

25.

We celebrate our first Christmas at sea – or at least, the English humans and bears of our party do, for the Russian crew prefer to wait until their laggard calendar produces the feast on January 6th. There is no dissension about this, as both parties are happy to have two festivals with as good a meal as can be provided at sea, and an extra rum ration to wash it down. It is also little Aeolus' first Christmas, though at barely two months old he is unaware of it. His hair is beginning to grow, and it is the same flaming red as his mother's.

It was a happy and convivial day interspersed with the daily routine of our voyage, now so familiar that we barely notice our duties and watches. Dolores intervened with the Russian cook to produce an acceptable plum pudding, which was served flaming with rum to the delight of all the crew. We remember our last Christmas, or Christmases, amid the luxurious hospitality of Count Bagarov – but here we are, still with the Count and on his own ship, and all present with the addition of one bear and one human baby, welcome visitors indeed.

We do not intend to make landfall until we reach the Cape of Good Hope, and will take an easterly course that will keep us well clear of the island of Madagascar. When sailing down the east coast of Africa it is advisable to stay well clear of the land, as the prevailing east winds have driven many a ship ashore and the coast is littered with wrecks. The region is also infested with pirates – not that we have any fear of them with our crew of bears, but tangling with them would only bring pointless delay and exertion.

Our intended course will take us past the Chagos islands and Mauritius, both in French hands. As far as we know, France and Russia are still allies in name, but we are unwilling to put that to the proof and will steer clear of them. On the advice of Misha, the only member of the crew who has sailed in these waters, we will also do well to avoid Madagascar which, he says, is visited only by pirates and slavers. He told us of a French gentleman who came to the island to study its fauna, which include the mysterious lemurs found only here. He vanished into the interior and was never heard of again.

January 1ᵗ, 1811.

We celebrate the New Year by crossing the Equator yet again, southbound for the Cape. Little Aeolus has now crossed the line three times and must be getting used to it. The rest of us drank to the continued success of our voyage in rum. And, now I think of it, so did Aeolus, at second hand from Dolores. He sleeps well and is mostly cheerful when awake, all that one could expect in one so young.

January 6ᵗʰ, 1811.

Today, of course, is 25th December in the old calendar, and our second Christmas. It is good to have these continuing festivities to punctuate the tedium of a long voyage. Count Bagarov made a long speech in Russian which was cheered by all, but I cannot recollect what it was about.

January 13ᵗʰ, 1811.

The last of our feasts at the turn of the seasons, the Russian New Year – not so new for the English members of the crew, but another cause for celebration. And there is another reason to celebrate: Beaivi is due to bear a cub. The voyage has thrown the customary seasons of polar bears askew, but we expect a birth early in May, by which time we hope to be in whatever part of Europe Fate takes us to.

February 1ˢᵗ, 1811.

After reaching the safe latitude of 32 degrees south we have been able to turn west without the risk of being driven ashore on the barren African coast. This afternoon, to our relief, we sighted land in the distance, and with a fair wind we should reach Cape Town tomorrow.

February 2ⁿᵈ, 1811.

As we approached Cape Town from the east we saw a vessel approaching from the west, evidently heading for the same port. After some hours we could discern the fine lines of a Royal Navy frigate in full sail, tacking into the east wind while our slower craft was coasting in, so that we arrived at the same time. It was clear from the telescopes pointed at us that they were curious about what was obviously a naval vessel flying the Russian flag (but not the Russian naval ensign) so far from her home.

We sailed side by side into the harbour, within hailing distance. The captain of the other ship introduced himself: Sextus Whimbrel, of H.M.S. *Intolerable*, on his way from London to Bombay.

The Count leaned over the taffrail and raised his megaphone: 'Cheerio, me deario, an' I'm Count Bagarov o' the good ship *Dronning*

Bengjerd. In the nime o' 'is Imperial Majesty, Emperor o' all the Russias, we bin on a voyage o' exploration, an' we gone through the Norf-East Passage – nah we're 'omeward bahnd the long way.'

We were close enough to see from the reaction of the captain and the men around him that we were not believed, and my acute ears caught one of the British seamen muttering 'Pull the other one, it's got bloody bells on it.' It was not just the improbability of our story of a voyage never before achieved: the Count's villainous accent and, it has to be said, his name when pronounced in the correct Russian manner, were detrimental to belief.

This was the first time that we realised that our tale might be incredible. The astute Stamford Raffles in Batavia had accepted it without demur, but then we were still quite far to the east and the notion of our having emerged from the Bering Strait seemed likely enough. Whether we are believed or not, others will make the voyage later. Echoing Horace, I say *Credite posteri*, Believe me, ye who come after.

As we dropped anchor side by side in the harbour of Cape Town, and our well drilled band of bears furled the topsails a good two minutes more quickly than the British sailors could achieve – and in particular, as two huge polar bears could be seen on deck hauling in the clewlines – we sensed a growing respect from the other party.

Before the harbourmaster's boat headed towards us, bringing the usual tiresome requests for dues and chores, the Count had invited Captain Whimbrel aboard to take a glass of wine with him. In the event it was three bottles of claret, almost the last of our cellar, but they were well invested, for by the time the captain clambered a shade unsteadily down the rope ladder to return to his own vessel our tale was fully believed and our exploits acclaimed.

However, I fear we shall face further incredulity in the future.

The captain brought us news of our old friend Sir Arthur Wellesley. He is now Viscount Wellington, apparently taking his title from a small town in Somerset with which, as far as any of us knew, he has no connection, but it has a fine sound. I once performed there in the old days of touring with Fred, and it was a sleepy little spot. The Viscount has been giving the French a hard pounding in Spain and Portugal, but the affair is by no means settled yet.

February 4ᵗʰ, 1811.

On our travels we have visited places that were administered by the British East India Company, but the Cape Province is under direct British rule, having been taken over from the Dutch in 1806 to prevent its falling into French hands. The British government shows no willingness to return this beautiful and fertile land to its former owners. Indeed, the administration has treated the settlers with some hostility, outlawing the use of Dutch as an official language. In consequence many of these people have quit the province, going to other regions where there are more of their countrymen. Those that are left are resentful of their new overlords.

The natives are also in motion. Formerly this land was inhabited by the Khoikhoi, a people somewhat different from the conventional idea of Africans, as they are relatively light-skinned and have a slightly Oriental cast of countenance. They are nomadic cattle herders and live in hemispherical tents similar to those that one of our sailors has seen in Mongolia, to the east of Russia, where the local name for them is *yurt*.

In recent years these people have retreated before the advance of another people, also cattle herders, whose name I cannot properly set down on paper. The nearest I can render it is Kosa, but the consonant I have represented as K is a peculiar click that defies both description and utterance. They are darker and more typically African in their appearance.

The natives seem resigned to European occupation, though there is a good deal of cattle theft. However, I cannot avoid feeling that a land where four nations are jostling for position cannot remain peaceful for long, and that sooner or later smouldering ill feeling will erupt into violence.

February 5ᵗʰ, 1811.

Our ramblings took us to Simon's Town, on the east side of the Cape peninsula and named after a former Dutch governor, Simon van der Stel. Here we met Captain Whimbrel again, for the town now houses a British naval base to which he had moved his ship in order to have some minor repairs performed.

We also met, to our astonishment, a flock of penguins on the beach. None of us had ever seen this flightless bird of the Southern Ocean before, and had no idea that their realm extended so far to the north. However, as the old proverb has it, Ἀεὶ φέρει τι Λιβύη καινόν, Africa always brings something new. This must be the first time that a polar bear has encountered a penguin – or at least a southern penguin, for the name was originally applied to a different bird, the Great Auk of the north Atlantic, which has now been hunted almost to extinction.

Never having seen a bear before, they showed no fear of us, and Boris and Beaivi swam among them. They reported that the creatures, so comically ungainly on land, could travel with astonishing speed under water, propelling themselves with their wings which resemble the flippers of a seal. Boris said that he had tactfully refrained from trying to eat any of them; but if he had wished to, he would have had a devil of a time catching these swift fowls as they fly gracefully through the deep.

February 7ᵗʰ, 1811.

We are at sea again. Our plan is to take a westerly course home, a longer route but probably a faster one as the winds will be more favourable once we have recrossed the line, for they blow roughly in a clockwise circle in the North Atlantic. Also, the African coast is as dangerous to sailors on its west side as it is on the east, and all should heed the old adage,

Take care, beware
The Bight of Benin.
One comes out
Though forty go in.

We plan to make our next landfall in Brazil, probably at Recife on the eastern tip of the South American continent. It would be a pity to conclude so long and wide a voyage without visiting America, a continent to which no one on board has ventured before, though we passed within a few miles of one of its less hospitable regions when we came through the Bering Strait.

26.

Late last night, as we were heading north-west in a moderate wind, a tremendous grinding crash threw the whole ship askew, and we found ourselves drifting with the sails flapping dangerously, threatening to take us aback. The wheel spun useless, with no effect on the rudder. We were all on deck in a moment and Master Ulyanov, capably surveying our plight, ordered all the sails on the mizen mast to be taken in, so that without steering at least we were heading steadily downwind.

This done, we peered over the stern to see what had happened to the rudder. It was completely gone, and when we lowered a boat to inspect the damage we found that the lower pintle – that is, the hinge of the rudder – had been ripped from the sternpost, taking a large piece of timber with it.

The impact had also started at least one plank, and the ship was leaking rapidly. We bound a sail over the hole – what a comfort it is to have such strong swimmers as our polar bears Boris and Beaivi at these times! – and pumped the bilges dry, a task that took us some hours. Finally we were safe enough; but as Anacharsis wisely observed, Τέτταρας δακτύλους θανάτου οἱ πλέοντες ἀπέχουσιν, Those who go to sea are four inches from death.

The immediate danger averted, we had time to think of what had happened, and what we should do. Almost certainly a whale had surfaced under the stern; I hope it was less injured by the collision than our vessel.

There was no possibility of replacing the rudder at sea. We had enough spare timber to cobble up a jury rudder, but the damage to the sternpost would have made it impossible to attach it. Therefore we had to adopt an ancient recourse, a steering oar. The carpenter made us one from the largest spare spar and some planks bound on with iron hoops, and fixed a tiller to the upper end. We lowered him over the starboard side of the stern in a sling, and he attached fixings to the hull and bound the oar to them securely. (I should mention that the oar must go on the starboard side – that is, the 'steerboard' side – because it is easier for a right-handed steersman to work it there.)

The oar proved effective and surprisingly easy to turn because, unlike a rudder, it was balanced fore and aft on its shaft and had no drag forcing it to the centre. On the other hand it could never be let go, because it had to be held straight to keep the ship on a straight course, so it required constant vigilance on the part of the helmsman.

We could not complete our planned course to Recife in this condition, so we headed for the nearest port, Rio de Janeiro, where we could have the ship properly repaired.

February 28th, 1811.

We reached Rio without further incident and anchored in the harbour. Fred, Jem and myself took a boat ashore to find a shipyard. Of course after our experiences in the war they both have fluent Portuguese, and I can understand and write it with the slate that I always carry on a cord around my neck. It is wonderful how having a bear as a party to the negotiations assures us a reasonable estimate for the work.

Having found what seemed a satisfactory arrangement, we returned to the waterfront. As we arrived a melancholy sight met our eyes: a slave ship had arrived, and the unfortunate Africans were being taken ashore in boats, each one with an overseer brandishing a whip and a pistol. The slaves, who had been packed together like skeletons in a charnel house, were emaciated and stinking, and the blank despair in their eyes told of their treatment.

Their initial abduction from their homeland is often carried out by their own people for a trifling financial inducement, though usually Arab slave traders have a hand in the business. But the ships that carry them over, killing many on the way through disease, are manned by Europeans – in this case Portuguese, though under Napoleon the French have regained an important role in the trade.

Angelina, a bear who knows what it is like to be chained and whipped, was so incensed by the spectacle that we had to hold her back from running at an overseer and ripping him to shreds – as he doubtless deserved, though in the long run it would have achieved little.

Now, before I make myself look high-minded in condemning the behaviour of foreigners, let us remember that, while slavery was never tolerated in Britain and there is a longstanding tradition under common law of freeing any slaves found in our islands, the trading of slaves in the colonies has been outlawed only since 1807, and even now those found guilty of it are fined only a sum that they can well afford. When we were in Cape Town, Captain Whimbrel told us that Mr Henry Brougham was attempting to bring a bill through parliament that would greatly increase the penalties, but the fact remains that British sugar plantations in the West Indies are still using – if no longer trading – slaves, or sometimes indentured labourers who are no more than slaves under another name.

Brazil too has an important sugar trade, and for this slaves are brought in and sold openly and legally, and the miserable Africans we saw were destined for profitable sale to plantation owners, and profitable labour till they died. The region also produces coffee, and gold and diamonds have been found; the labour for all these industries is conducted by slaves. We cannot alter this, but it cast a sad shadow over our visit to this handsome city, where we are destined to pass some time while our ship is set to rights.

Strange as it may seem, Rio is now the capital city of Portugal and the seat of the Portuguese king John (or João in Portuguese) the Sixth, who fled with all his court when the Corsican tyrant's army marched into his country. He and his entourage are now guests here, to the satisfaction neither of the Cariocas – a native name for the settlers in Rio – nor of the luckless Portuguese, as we know from our own experience of fighting beside them.

To further scale the heights of absurdity, the government in exile has set up a military academy in the city, which gives a futile semblance of warlike intention – as Phaedrus put it, *trepide concursans, occupta in otio*, a people rushing hastily to and fro, busy with idleness – while the battle against the invaders of their country is conducted by Lord Wellington's forces and the motley bands of peasants with both of whom we had the honour to serve.

March 2ⁿᵈ, 1811.

Our battered vessel is now careened in the shipyard while her stern is repaired. It is remarkable how much damage she sustained from this chance encounter, and most fortunate for us that her heavy construction held her together while we limped ashore. The sternpost is split for most of its length, and the foreman told us that it will need to be entirely replaced. Even the Count baulked at the cost of this operation; but after considering the value of the cargo we carry – to which he proposes to add a quantity of Brazilian coffee – he decided that this was no time to abandon our gallant old tub. Nevertheless, with the artisans working at all the speed that his wealth can procure, it will be at least a fortnight before she is seaworthy again and we can be on our way.

Meanwhile, the crew are sampling all the delights that a prosperous port can afford them. I am glad that we had the foresight to purchase some of the Chinese remedies for venereal diseases that we found in Canton. But these will not guard them from broken heads suffered in brawls in the many places of entertainment that are to be found here.

March 4ᵗʰ, 1811.

Leaving the sailors to their diversions, the Count, Fred, Jem and all the bears have been exploring the countryside around the city. Much of it is now given to agriculture for the support of the city, but there are still broad tracts of undisturbed forest inhabited by the local tribes. The most numerous of these are the Aimoré or Botocudos, the latter name being a Portuguese one referring to their strange practice of distending their lower lips by the insertion of wooden discs, giving them a hideous duck-billed appearance which they deem attractive. They enlarge the lobes of their ears in a similar manner. The encroachment of Europeans on their lands is much reducing their numbers, a process speeded, sad to say, by the deliberate spreading of smallpox among them, a disease to which the natives have no resistance whatever.

We made small presents of knives, mirrors and beads to them, and were permitted to wander their lands unmolested, though they can have no fondness for white men. They showed no amazement at the presence

of bears in our party; probably they thought that we were just another European tribe. We danced for them, and they for us, establishing a bond between nations deeper than the petty politicking of rulers.

We have recruited a guide named Moema, of the Tabajara people, to show us the wonders of the untamed woods that still lie within a few hours' walk of the capital, despite the efforts of farmers to subdue this fertile land.

The country teems with strange birds. Even when we were in the harbour at Rio we could see black fork-tailed frigatebirds circling on huge pointed wings, seeking whatever food they could find – though strangely these coastal birds never come down on water, unlike our familiar gulls. The city is populated by black vultures on the lookout for the dead creatures that always lie around the roads, and they perform the task of cleaners in a place where no man will raise a hand to clear his street of corpses.

In the forest we saw parrots of all kinds, from small but loud-voiced green parakeets to huge dark blue macaws. In the more open areas there are small owls, akin to the little owls that live around the Mediterranean Sea but with the peculiar habit of nesting in underground burrows made by other animals. They hunt small prey by running rapidly over the ground on their long strong legs.

The most remarkable bird we saw was the toucan, whose huge curved bill is almost as large as its body. This cumbersome-looking organ assists them in reaping the abundant fruit that hangs on the trees of this so far unravaged paradise. In the words of Euripides, Μεταβολὴ παντῶν γλυκεῖα, The variety of all things is a pleasure.

There are also beasts aplenty, including the capybara, which is said to be of the rat kind but is the size of a small pig. They roam the forest in herds. We caught and consumed some of them, and they were capital eating. Once we had a distant sight of a jaguar, a great spotted cat resembling a leopard. They are considered sacred by the natives – but, as we bears know only too well, sacredness does not save one from being hunted.

March 21st, 1811.

The *Dronning Bengjerd* is afloat again, as good as ever she was – she may not be swift, but she has the strength of a true bear – and we are heading up the coast at a safe distance from land since the prevailing wind is from the south-east. The hold is full of sacks of coffee beans, we have fresh provisions, and our hearts are high as we head for home. There are still two thousand miles to sail before our final northward crossing of the Equator, but we have already done that so many times that it is no more significant to us than sauntering across the street to buy a cabbage. Once we are back in our own hemisphere, not all the fabled storms of the North Atlantic shall keep us from or beloved shore.

27.

Our wanderings have brought us to Trinidad, the largest and almost the easternmost of the chain of islands which dot the edge of the Caribbean Sea. Skirting the western edge of the island, we dropped anchor in the harbour of the capital town, Port of Spain. As its name suggests, this was once a Spanish colony, but the British invaded at a time when Spain was allied with the Corsican tyrant – how alliances shift! – and secured permanent possession under the Treaty of Amiens in 1802; they have no intention of returning it to our present allies.

Going ashore, we found the place to be an indescribable hotchpotch of peoples: Spanish colonists, Frenchmen fleeing the revolution who first sought refuge in Haiti and were then driven out by the bloody insurrection there, newly arrived British settlers, elderly pirates of all nations who have settled down on their ill-gotten wealth, a few of the original natives though most of them shun towns, and of course the inevitable sad population of African slaves though there are fewer of them here than in Rio. Yet all is reasonably harmonious, for this is a rich island, and wealth brings civil order.

April 25ᵗʰ, 1811.

In the afternoon we visited an inn – or at least a shack where drink was served – to sample a local beverage called 'punch', a name which I believe to be derived from the Hindustani word *panj*, five, because it is made from five ingredients, rum, lime juice, sugar, water and spices such as nutmeg. It is refreshing enough, though not to be compared with good English ale which, God willing, we shall soon enough be drinking again.

As we sat peacefully imbibing, under the awed gaze of the local people for it is not often that eleven bears visit an inn, there was a shout of '*Les voilà, ces sales cons d'ours!*' Looking towards the sound, I saw a dozen men rising unsteadily to their feet and reaching for weapons, mostly the crude cutlasses used to cut sugar cane, but also a couple of pistols. I recognised them as the survivors of the crew of the *Incroyable*, the French privateer that we captured two years ago.

There was no time for musing on this fortuitous encounter, so I threw the table at the two men with guns. As they fell, one pistol went off and the other clattered harmlessly into a corner. However, the impact knocked over another table, and its occupants sprang vengefully to their feet. In no time the entire company, inflamed with rum, were belabouring each other with fists and furniture.

We devoted ourselves to disabling the privateersmen, a simple enough task though we took care not to deal any of them a fatal blow. Bruin laid three low with a chair before it fell apart in his paws, and the last of them was dispatched by Dolores, with little Aeolus cradled with one hand and a rum bottle in the other. She would make a good bear.

Soon enough the scene was quiet apart from the groans of the fallen; the less battered had left. The landlord surveyed his smashed premises with practised gloom, but a few silver thalers from the Count lightened his mood, and we helped him throw the inert patrons out of the door. I am sure that the inn was open for business again by sundown, and I am equally sure that no one in Port of Spain will raise a hand to us for the duration of our visit.

April 29th, 1811.

While we we were in the town the Count heard of a wondrous natural phenomenon, a lake of black tar at the south-west corner of the island. He was determined to view it, so we have sailed a short distance to the south and anchored near Point Fortin, a small village surrounded by plantations of cocoa and coconuts. The lake was a short walk to the east of where we landed.

I suppose that we were expecting a picturesque inferno of black boiling tar and sulphurous fumes, but I have to say that the spectacle was a disappointing one – an expanse of ponds and swamps surrounded by stunted plants, and the only remarkable thing the crusts of asphalt that littered the scene, weathered to an inconspicuous grey colour.

Slaves were loading the substance on to carts. They told us that we should never stand still for more than a moment on this treacherous surface, for fear that the viscous tar would slowly give way and we should sink into it to be lost for ever. We were more than happy to take their advice, and paused only for long enough to gather some of the tar.

This is asphalt, the substance mentioned by Herodotus as having been used in the building of the walls of Babylon, for it is exuded from the ground in that region. I had brought with me the Count's copy of this splendid book, even now useful to travellers who might profit from its advice on such matters as the catching of crocodiles, and when we were back on the ship I looked up the passage.

Δεῖ δή με πρὸς τούτοισι ἔτι φράσαι ἵνα τε ἐκ τῆς τάφρου ἡ γῆ ἀναισιμώθη, καὶ τὸ τεῖχος ὅντινα τρόπον ἔργαστο. ὀρύσσοντες ἅμα τὴν τάφρον ἐπλίνθευον τὴν γῆν τὴν ἐκ τοῦ ὀρύγματος ἐκφερομένην, ἑλκύσαντες δὲ πλίνθους ἱκανὰς ὤπτησαν αὐτὰς ἐν καμίνοισι· μετὰ δὲ τέλματι χρεώμενοι ἀσφάλτῳ θερμῇ καὶ διὰ τριήκοντα δόμων πλίνθου ταρσοὺς καλάμων διαστοιβάζοντες, ἔδειμαν πρῶτα μὲν τῆς τάφου τὰ χείλεα, δευτέρα δὲ αὐτὸ τὸ τεῖχος τὸν αὐτὸν τρόπον.

I must also say where the earth was used when it was dug from the moat, and how the wall was built. As they dug the moat, they made bricks of the clay that was brought out of the place they dug, and when they had shaped enough bricks they baked them in ovens; then, using hot asphalt as mortar and inserting layers of woven reeds at every thirtieth course of bricks, they built first the edge of the moat and then the wall itself in the same way.

Asphalt is also mentioned by Dioscorides and the elder Pliny, and more recently the French have discovered deposits in their own country, and use it for waterproofing walls and roofs. When we returned to our ship, we used the tar we had gathered to repair our two remaining ship's boats, both of which had begun to leak in consequence of being kept on deck and only used at long intervals, so that the wood had dried and shrunk. The asphalt melted quickly in a bucket over a small fire and was easy to apply. Master Ulyanov considered it superior to the Stockholm tar we had used before, made from the exudations of pine trees, and far better than the Chinese caulk of lime and tung oil that had been applied when our ship was in dock in Canton.

Before I leave the subject of this remarkable substance, I may say that its use would be an improvement to our roads which, no matter how carefully laid and smoothed, are soon rutted by the wheels of carts and coaches and washed away by rain. A coating of asphalt mixed with gravel would strengthen the surface and render it waterproof, and would also allay the clouds of choking dust that are raised when a road is traversed in dry weather. The same treatment would keep our city streets from turning into stinking quagmires whenever it rains.

However, there is one case in which the adoption of this useful substance has had unhappy results. The celebrated painter of portraits Sir Joshua Reynolds, who liked to set off his subjects with a dark background, adopted a mixture of asphalt and linseed oil as a convenient way of securing a deep black. It is said to have produced a fine effect when the paintings were new, but now, a mere nineteen years after his death, all these works have become seamed with cracks where the pigment has dried and shrunk and become grey – a shame, for he was a fine painter. Needless to say, the accident also infuriated the royal personages, nobles and wealthy citizens who had paid substantial sums to have themselves commemorated by this illustrious artist. A cruel rhyme was circulated,

When Sir Joshua Reynolds died,
All Nature was degraded:
The King dropped a tear into the Queen's ear,
And all his pictured faded.

May 5ᵗʰ, 1811.

On our way north again, with a fair breeze filling our by now grubby and patched sails. But we have all come to love our old tub and forgive her

vices, for she has kept us afloat in ice and storms and is now bearing us slowly homeward.

We missed Beaivi at supper, and after we had bolted down our monotonous diet of salt beef and sauerkraut, relieved by a generous tot of rum, we went to look for her. Small noises from the sail locker revealed her presence. My enquiring call was answered, and I opened the door – and there was Beaivi with a newborn cub, which she was carefully licking.

A brief digression: there is a foolish belief among humans that bear cubs are born in a shapeless state, and have to be licked into shape by their mother before they become recognisable bears. Indeed, there is a common expression, 'licking into shape', which refers to this supposed process.

As Suetonius wrote in his Life of Virgil,

Cum Georgica scriberet, traditur cotidie meditatos mane plurimos versus dictare solitus ac per totum diem retractando ad paucissimos redigere, non absurde carmen se more ursae parere dicens et lambendo demum effingere.

When he was writing the Georgics, it is said that he used to dictate every day a large number of lines which he had composed in the morning, and then spend the rest of the day reducing them to a very small number, wittily remarking that he made his poem in the manner of a she-bear, and gradually licked it into shape.

Needless to say, bear cubs are born small but perfectly formed; however, they do need careful cleaning so that their scanty new fur will resist the cold – especially so in the case of polar bears, whose cubs in natural conditions are born around Christmas in the northern chill.

We were all overjoyed by the sight, but only Dolores (with whose labour Beaivi had so well assisted) and myself went in cautiously, to avoid disturbing her privacy. Even Boris, the cub's father, was not welcome on the scene. We congratulated her and admired the little bear. In the words of Horace, *pulchre, bene, recte!* beautiful, good, perfect! Then, not wishing to disturb her further, we retired. But there was music and dancing on deck to celebrate the burgeoning of life on our lucky ship. Doubtless the new mother will have heard the noise and been cheered by it.

Yet how different are the ways of humans and bears! A human birth is attended by hours of appalling pain, and the bare survival or mother and child is in doubt throughout this long agony. A bear simply goes into a quiet place and, although as I know myself the birth is not without pain, it is quickly accomplished and swiftly followed by the joy of a new cub.

The little bear will not open her eyes for a month, and will not be active for a month after that. But compare the growth of human infants, who cannot even walk until they are a year or more old, and remain in a pitiable state of dependence for many years more, while a young bear will soon be at his full strength. Mother bears are famed for the fierceness with which they protect their cubs, but for patient endurance I have to hand the crown to humans.

May 7th, 1811.

The new cub will be called Marina, for she was born at sea. She has already met Aeolus, child of the storm, though I am not sure that they noticed one another, each one immersed in her or his private world. But we have many more miles to sail before we are home, and it will be interesting to see how these two little creatures come to understand each other.

If all goes as planned, our next landfall will be at New York in the United States. We are only too well aware of the worsening relations between Britain and America, and Fred and Jem have been rehearsing the part of Russian sailors named Fyodor and Yevgeny to avoid appearing conspicuous. Dolores can convincingly claim to be Irish on the grounds of her flaming red hair, although she was born in Bermondsey. She has not a word of Erse but neither do most of her pretended countrymen, for all their patriotic bluster.

28.

June 3rd, 1811.

The city of New York lies in a broad river estuary whose wooded slopes give no hint of what will appear around the corner. The river is divided into several channels, forming the island of Manhattan on whose south end the city stands.

We anchored in the harbour and went ashore in the ship's two boats, now cured of their leaks with a coating of Trinidad asphalt. The waterfront is adorned with handsome buildings that would grace any European city, and the quayside was bustling with every kind of activity, while a babel of most of the world's languages met our ears.

After the Count had transacted the usual business with the harbourmaster, he told us that, despite his Russian name, his London accent had raised some hackles. More than thirty years after the colonies broke

their ties with Britain, feelings are still running high. Indeed, in the present conflict Americans seem to be taking the side of the gimcrack tyranny of Napoleon, the very opposite of the ideals to which they claim to aspire.

Safe in our Russian nationality as long as we do not speak English, we repaired to a tavern and, while imbibing some lamentably bad whiskey apparently made from maize, listened to the local gossip. Two subjects were constantly mentioned.

First, the state of New York has recently abolished slavery, for which it is to be congratulated, but it has done so in a gradual way: the freed slaves have to serve a kind of apprenticeship, in which they remain indentured labourers paid a derisory wage, for some years before they become citizens. There are now many completely free Africans in the city, but I noticed that the only black faces were those of the tavern servants, and I surmise that it will be many years before they take a full part in the life of the district – if indeed they ever attain it. It is in the nature of any society to keep its lower ranks in their place but, if they are not provided with a ladder by which they can ascend, civil unrest invariably results.

Second, the municipal leaders have grand ambitions for their city. They expect it to spread northwards over the entire island, and to this end they have divided its surface into rectangular plots which are now being marked with inscribed boundary stones. This plan has aroused the ire of the many farmers in the north of the island, who expect to be expropriated and driven off their land with little compensation. While their plight may inspire a certain sympathy, let us not forget that the original natives of the island were expelled by the first Dutch settlers when in 1626 they bought Manhattan island from them for 24 dollars'

worth of trinkets and beads and a jug of the execrable spirit we were drinking.

May I add that American beer is but a pale shadow of the real article. The inhabitants have also tried making wine from the fox grape which grows wild here, so named because of its odour, with unhappy results.

June 5th, 1811.

The city presents an animated spectacle, to such an extent that one must take great care when crossing the broad and crowded streets to avoid being felled by a furiously driven wagon. The principal languages that one hears spoken, apart from English, are Dutch and German.

When we had purchased all those items we required for our continued voyage, we resolved to explore the country to the north, beyond the present limits of the city. It is a pleasant landscape of rolling hills, forests, clear streams and small farms, and it will be sad to see it swallowed up by the dreary rectangles of the planned streets whose cornerstones are everywhere to be seen.

We fell into conversation with an aged farmer, a Mr de Kuiper, whom we met leaning on the front gate of his property. He was surprised to see bears, he said; they had been plentiful in his youth but the coming of Europeans had driven them out completely. This saddened us, as we had hoped to meet some of our American cousins. There were also very few of the original human inhabitants, expelled in the same way. While the European incursion into Manhattan, and into the east coast of America

as a whole, may have begun as a colonial venture, it is now looking more like a complete replacement of the population by settlers of European stock, and of course their sad train of Africans brought in as slaves – and still such in reality, for all the boasts of emancipation.

It must be said that all civilisation depends on slave labour, or something like it. The prosperous lives of respectable citizens can be maintained only by hordes of miserable wretches toiling in the shadows, and paying these unfortunates a derisory wage does little to disguise their servile status. Even in famously free Britain we are sustained by labourers in the farms and mills working for a few shillings a week to supply our needs. Yet such is the way of all society, be it human or that of other animals: there must always be a hierarchy, and all worthy attempts to level it out end in failure.

On a more cheerful note, the joyous birth of Marina has had its consequences among the bears. My own dear Bruin has taken Angelina as his mate, and I am happy to say that she is already expecting a cub; and so is Peter's mate Emily. It is early yet, and both cubs will probably be born on land after we have finally reached home. God willing, I shall be a grandmother!

Despite all the varied distractions and adventures of our voyage, we are all longing to stand on our native soil again, be it in England or Russia. In the words that Homer put into the mouth of wandering Odysseus,

Ἀλλὰ καὶ ὣς ἐθέλω καὶ ἐέλδομαι ἤματα πάντα
οἴκαδέ τ᾿ ἐλθέμεναι καὶ νόστιμον ἦμαρ ἰδέσθαι.
εἰ δ᾿ αὖ τις ῥαίῃσι θεῶν ἐνὶ οἴνοπι πόντῳ,
τλήσομαι ἐν στήθεσσιν ἔχων ταλαπενθέα θυμόν·
ἤδη γὰρ μάλα πολλὰ πάθον καὶ πολλὰ μόγησα
κύμασι καὶ πολέμῳ· μετὰ καὶ τόδε τοῖσι γενέσθω.

But every day I wish and yearn to reach
My home, and see the day of my return.
And if some god should smite me on the sea,
I will endure it, for my heart is strong.
Already I have suffered and toiled much
At sea and in the war; add this to that.

June 7ᵗʰ, 1811.

Last night Anton, one of the ordinary seamen, returned excitedly to the ship with the news that he had found a proper Russian tavern frequented by Russian sailors, with not a word of English spoken on the premises. We resolved to visit it this evening, and he led us to the east end of the city, accompanied by the entire crew except the unhappy ones whose turn it was to keep watch on the vessel, and even those we reduced to a minimum.

And there it was: a wooden sign bearing the legend Волжская Таверна, The Volga Tavern, in Russian – but not in English – led us down a flight of rickety stairs into a basement from which sounds of merriment emerged, mingled with the music of fiddles and *balalaikas*.

The entry of a nobleman in a fine suit trimmed with gold braid, two dozen bearded and rough-looking sailors, a young woman with flaming red hair carrying a small child, eleven bears and a cub provoked no more than a moment of interest before the patrons returned to their pursuits. True Russians expect the unexpected.

We found tables in a corner and purchased several bottles of what we found to be very good *vodka*, a delightful discovery after the Americans'

unfortunate attempt at distilling spirits. Dolores and Beaivi, mindful of the welfare of their infants, preferred beer and even this, they said, far surpassed the pitiful brew sold elsewhere in the city. We sat at our ease and listened to the patrons as they boasted about their adventures at sea and their conquests of women (of whom the few present seemed to be available for ready money with little wooing required).

After a few minutes their natural curiosity asserted itself, and a few sailors drifted across to our tables and asked who we were and whence we hailed. The imposing figure of Count Bagarov, who alone among our motley band struck a fine figure, awed them a little, but when he told them that we had come to New York by the North-East Passage and the circumnavigation of Asia, there were politely raised eyebrows.

Fred (or I should say Fyodor) broke in with his now fluent but ungrammatical Russian, 'We couldn't've done it without the bears. Did you see how they manned the ship when we came into harbour?'

Some of them had seen our superbly drilled taking in and furling of the sails, and there were grudging nods. Seizing the moment, I took my slate and wrote on it, Кроме того, мы не обычные медведи. Мы можем танцевать так, чтобы удивить всех вас – *Besides, we are no ordinary bears. We can dance so as to astonish you all.*

That really did command their attention. The Count signalled for some tables to be pushed back. Jem took out his flute and Fred borrowed a violin from the bandleader. Then we launched into our well practised routine, choosing the quicker dances that would appeal to a tavern audience. When we came to the culminating *gopak*, the band joined in to the familiar melody while everyone else ecstatically clapped their hands. As the bears subsided gratefully back on to their benches, the applause and cheering were deafening.

We mingled with our hosts and toasted them in more *vodka* – it was no occasion for remaining sober. The foreign accents of Fred, Jem and Dolores excited polite comment, but when they told the story of how Fred had been sentenced to hang in a corrupt trial, and how Jem and Dolores had snatched him from his fate, a wave of sympathy and understanding swept across the company. No doubt many of them have had their own troubles with the authorities. Now we were all Russian brothers and sisters for life.

I should mention at this point that Fred (or Fyodor) and Jem (or Yevgeny) are very different in appearance from the neat, nondescript Englishmen who set out for St Petersburg. Both are hirsute and tanned by wind and weather to the colour of mahogany; and Fred, with a flowing grey beard, looks like one of the Old Testament prophets in an Italian religious painting. Dressed in the last patched and ill fitting remnants of what the ship's slop chest could furnish, they present a magnificently ruffianly appearance. Even were Fred to stroll past the Old Bailey in London, where the officers of the law are no doubt still eager to apprehend him, they would not have the slightest idea of his identity.

I am not entirely sure how we made our way back to the ship, but I remember a moment when the city watchmen appeared on the scene and seemed to be taking exception to our unsteady singing, roaring company as we lurched through the streets, only to fall back as a phalanx of bears surged to the front. I am a little surprised that I have still been able to write an account of the evening's adventures, but now I shall subside gratefully into my bunk. Tomorrow we shall haul up the anchor and depart on the last leg of our homeward voyage.

29.

June 9th, 1811.

At sea once more, we discovered that two of our crew had deserted, preferring the fleshpots of New York to their homeland and what will certainly be a more than generous reward from our patron Count Bagarov. These are the first two to have 'jumped ship', as sailors put it – though it has to be said that our previous ports of call have offered less attractive prospects. Still, they were only two and we can get on well enough without them. As for our loyal remainder, in the words of Virgil, *Cuncti adsint, meritaeque expectent praemia palmae*, Let all be present and await the rewards of the well deserved accolade.

June 20th, 1811.

An uneventful voyage so far, if any crossing of the wild North Atlantic may be called uneventful. At least there have been no serious storms and the sails and rigging remain intact. We have become such hardened sea bears that we barely notice any weather short of a hurricane.

Marina is the most beautiful little white bear cub imaginable, and the darling of the entire crew. It will not be long before she surpasses Aeolus, seven months her senior – how slowly human infants grow up! One of the sailors, Yuri, is a passable painter, and has been making portraits of us all, singly and together. We are aware that the time is no longer far off when we must abandon the brotherhood of the ship in which we have lived for so long, and go our separate ways. It is a sad prospect but an inevitable one; as Heraclitus said, Πάντα ῥεῖ, Everything flows.

July 5ᵗʰ, 1811.

We had our first sight of England at dawn: the Lizard Point in Cornwall. Shortly afterwards were were hailed by a frigate of His Majesty's navy, HMS *Spiteful*, and ordered to heave to. It was clear that they suspected us of being blockade runners, despite our flying the flag of a neutral nation, Russia. We obeyed as we must, and were boarded by a gold-braided gentleman who introduced himself as Captain Fotherington.

We had determined to make matters as difficult for him as we could, so we affected to have no speakers of English on board. As the captain came up over the side, he was daunted by finding himself passing a gauntlet of bears, five to a side, to be confronted by the equally magnificently attired Count Bagarov, and the looming figure of Captain Ulyanov who addressed him in barbarous French, a language of neither party had much command. But the threat that *Sa Majesté Impériale de toutes les Russies* would be seriously displeased if Fotherington pressed his enquiries too closely, and that this might provoke *un incident diplomatique*, had the desired effect, and he retired without insisting on searching the ship. We were indeed carrying some quantity of goods that would incur a heavy duty in England: tea from Canton and rum and tobacco from Trinidad.

The encounter gave Fred an idea. 'Right,' he said. 'We bin through the blockade. Reckon it's time to do a little tradin'.' The Count happily agreed, and nightfall found us anchored off the coast of the Cotentin peninsula of Normandy, where Fred happened to know someone in the little village of Maupertus. This person, whose name I never discovered, provided us with forty barrels of French brandy, purchased with the Count's apparently endless fund of silver thalers.

July 6ᵗʰ, 1811.

Daybreak saw us sailing briskly north-west towards Eype, the little Dorset village where we had had some unlicensed dealings two years before, and we anchored off the coast shortly after sunset and sent a boat ashore, rowed by four bears and carrying Fred, Jem and myself. The local people remembered us, especially the bears, and we were warmly welcomed and had no difficulty in finding our former partners in trade at an inn. A bargain was swiftly transacted, and we had our goods ashore soon after midnight and were on our way again. How swiftly business can be conducted when no wearisome officials stand in the way!

The Count realised a handsome profit on the day's dealings. For all his aristocratic airs, he does not turn up his nose at financial gain. As the emperor Vespasian remarked when his son Titus delicately reprimanded him for profiting by the installation of public lavatories in Rome, *Pecunia non olet*, Money does not smell.

July 7ᵗʰ, 1811.

Alas! Good things must come to an end. Fred, Jem and I had decided that we must part with Count Bagarov in a place well to the west of London where, after all, Fred is still sought as an escaped criminal. Accordingly, we anchored at Bournemouth, a town small enough for us to avoid the attention of the forces of law but large enough for the recruitment of some sailors to man the ship on her continued voyage – though, as the Count tearfully said, 'Nuffink can replace yer bears. Yer bin good to me, and I won't forget yer.' We shall take a small portrait of him with us, executed by Yuri on a piece of oak plank.

Our company of bears must also divide, for Boris, Beaivi and little Marina are going on with the Count to find a home in Archangel. Our hearts are wrenched by parting. We hugged each other as only bears can.

Indeed the good Count did not forget us. As we went ashore for the last time he pressed into Fred's hands a heavy leather bag which we later found to contain the truly princely sum of £1000, much of it in English sovereigns from the previous day's transaction. His noble generosity is made even more apparent by the fact that he gave us no opportunity to thank him for his munificence as he surely deserved. How we shall miss his genial presence as he encouraged us through ice and storms!

July 8ᵗʰ, 1811.

We passed our first night on land in a small wood outside the town. It was strange not to feel the motion of a ship or to hear the groan of the shifting timbers, the creaking of the rigging and the rattling of blocks. But it was a warm night, and the stars overhead reminded us comfortingly that we were still in the same world.

After a breakfast of rabbits and an incautious fox washed down with some rum we had brought from the ship, while Dolores nursed Aeolus under an oak tree we sat down and debated what to do. We now had enough money to settle down if we wished, but nowhere to do so. Yet it was summer and it would be easy to adopt our old nomadic life until we found a spot that suited us. We resolved to head west, simply to put as much distance between London and ourselves as possible.

In the evening we found ourselves in Milton Abbas, a strange village consisting of identical thatched cottages disposed at equal intervals along a straight road, with a uniform horse chestnut tree between each one. We found an inn, which was off the alignment and did not seem part of the plan, and gave our customary performance, collecting a trifling amount from the local folk, which we scarcely needed – but if people are willing to pay to be entertained, they will appreciate the entertainment all the more.

Afterwards, the strange conformation of the village was explained to us. Thirty years ago there had been a village named Middleton nearby. However, the landlord, one Joseph Damer, Lord Middleton and Earl of Dorchester, had recently completed his large residence, which was visible not far away – an absurd construction of bulky blocks in the classical style superficially transformed to a parody of the medieval by the addition of pointed windows and a trimming along the top which was halfway between battlements and balustrades. This nobleman felt that the village was spoiling his view, and had it moved to a new site, razing the old buildings to the ground. While the relocated villagers mocked their landlord's vanity, they had to concede that their new dwellings were more comfortable than their old quarters.

July 11ᵗʰ, 1811.

This evening, having crossed from Dorset into Somerset, we arrived in the small market town of Wiveliscombe. It is not a place of commanding grandeur, and indeed the houses seem somewhat dilapidated. However, the locality is made more fragrant by the presence of a brewery, whose ventilated storehouses and smoking chimneys we observed as we entered the town.

In a street a short way to the north of the market square we saw the broad gateway of a coaching inn, and a sign proclaiming its name – The Bear. Naturally we went in at once. The owner did not seem disturbed by the arrival of eight eponymous creatures, and reached for eight pewter quart mugs hanging on the wall above him. I should mention that young Henry is no longer a little bear, and is as large as any of us; the days when a discerning landlord would offer him a mere pint are long gone.

Fred, Jem and Dolores were judged worthy only of pint mugs, and our host busied himself with filling them from a barrel behind the counter – Joseph Bramah's newfangled 'beer engine' for drawing beer up from the cellar has not yet reached Wiveliscombe.

The ale was remarkably good – deep brown, nutty in flavour, well hopped and strong. Aeolus will sleep well tonight. Fred complimented the proprietor on his brew, and asked him if it came from the local brewery.

'Ar,' he replied. 'That be Will Hancock's works. 'E's bin brewin' in Wilscum (for so he pronounced the name of the town) for quoite a few

years now. Truth to say, 'is ale be good enough. But Oi prefers to brew me own, the way Oi loikes it.' He motioned use to the other side of the room, and through the back window we saw a yard with the apparatus of a small brewery. He opened a window and an enticing malty scent drifted in.

There were not many other patrons to serve – indeed fewer than the quality of his ale seemed to merit – and his demeanour was visibly tinged with melancholy. We drifted into conversation with him. He is called Cornelius Boggins. He has been a widower for fifteen years and had intended to pass the ownership of the inn and brewery to his only son Jasper, but Jasper had imprudently enlisted in the army and had been killed in the bloody storming of Badajoz in April, and now he found himself without heir or prospects.

Fred and Jem told him of our exploits of the war in Spain and Portugal, and related their experience of the atrocities of that cruel campaign, and we fell into a sad sympathy. But as we talked, I sensed that an idea was forming in their minds, as indeed it was in mine.

While Mr Boggins was drawing ale for some men who had just arrived, and sending a serving maid to fetch food for them, we conferred. Fred spoke first: ''Ow d'yer like the idea o' buyin' this place? Reckon we could give it a go?'

'I always fancied the idea o' bein' an innkeeper,' said Jem.

'Reckon I could cope wiv the cookin',' Dolores said. 'Not too 'ard in a place like this, wiv a couple o' gals to 'elp me.'

I wrote on my slate, 'I would like to try my paw at brewing.'

When four kindred spirits come to the same conclusion there is no need for further conference. We waited only until Mr Boggins had finished serving his customers before we approached him. Nor did he seem surprised by our offer to purchase his establishment, saying only, 'When Oi seed all them bears come in the door, Oi knew it were the workin's o' the good Lord. 'E taketh away, but 'e giveth. 'Ow much are yer offerin'?'

Without overmuch haggling we settled on the sum of £250 for the building, a rambling place of some size, and another £250 for the goodwill of the business, with the condition that Mr Boggins should stay on until he had fully instructed us in the arts of innkeeping and brewing. This he was more than happy to accept, and it was cheering to see how his melancholy face brightened at the prospect of being able to pass down his skills.

We shall do our best to compensate him for the loss of his son. Also, I believe that our skill in providing entertainment will bring a flood of custom to our inn. And I shall be a brewing bear! I have mastered many arts, and I am eagerly looking forward to learning a new one.

30.

I have been too much occupied to keep up my diary for several months. We have all been toiling on the improvement of the Bear Inn, which had fallen into some disrepair since Cornelius had been widowed. But now the rooms are newly painted and furnished and spotlessly clean, and should Royalty chance to honour us with their presence, they would not find fault in our accommodation.

By the way, on our return we discovered that our good King George's madness has been pronounced to be incurable, sad to hear for he was a true lover of his country and a patron of the sciences and agriculture. The Prince of Wales, *de facto* regent for some years, has now been officially confirmed in that position by an Act of Parliament.

But enough of these mundane topics, for my true reason for taking up my pen again is that both Angelina and Emily have been safely delivered of cubs within three days of each other. Both are male. Angelina and Bruin have named theirs Arthur, after Viscount Wellington at whose side they fought in Spain and Portugal. Peter and Emily have called their cub Frederick, of course after our dear Fred who has guided us so well in our adventures, and who has stood as godfather to both cubs.

And I am a grandmother! It is such a joy to hold my dearest little grandbear. I cannot truthfully say that he resembles either of his parents, for newborn bear cubs do not look much like anything except what they

are, which is delightful in its own way. The same might be said of human infants, but humans are prone to sentimental delusions and will swear that their offspring are the image of their father or mother.

I am gaining skill as a brewer and have already devised an ale much to my taste and that of the other bears, dark with roasted barley and considerably stronger than the usual brew. We sell it as Brown Bear Ale, but its nickname among the human patrons is Old Staggers.

Although our customers often become merry, there is little fighting in our inn. People have learnt that if they become unruly, a bear will throw them out with a force that carries them across the street and into a patch of nettles on the other side.

December 26th, 1811.

Our first Christmas in Wiveliscombe has been a joyous occasion, with feasting and rejoicing in the true old English style. In the morning we attended the service at the ancient and tumbledown church of St Andrew, where there is no longer any surprise at seeing bears among the congregation, and Fred and Jem often assist the musicians. We closed the inn for the day, for everyone who has a home would be there with the family, but we remembered the unfortunate inhabitants of the workhouse and brought them in for a good dinner.

We drank the health our noble patron Count Bagarov with particular affection, for on Christmas Eve we had received a letter from him, replying to the letter we had sent him in July thanking him for his generosity on our long voyage. It takes a long while for letters to arrive in Archangel, and to return from there. We had politely written our letter in passable Russian, penned by my own paw. He returned the courtesy by writing to us in English of a sort, as follows.

My deer Fred Djem Doloris Daisy an all the barez,

I carnt tell yu ow delited I wer to reseave yur letter. Pleez du not thank me for the muny i giv yer, wich wer no mor than wot yu all diservd for yur loyl companyunship on our long voyidj. No dowt yu will be plesd to ear that Boris Beaivi an Marina are all in gud spiritz an they send gretinz an luv to yu all. I ope yur new cubz is doin well.

We reechd Arkhangelsk in gud order and sadly i sold our ole ship wot as carried us so far tho i wer pleezd to mayk a profit on the sayl. I also got a lot o wedj from the cargow of spicez an all thoz fingz wot we braut bak. I never thaut this voyidj wud be profitabl but it az bin. May other Russianz profit by our eksampl!

But ive ad an ard time convinsin peepl that we reely went fru the Norf Eestern Pasidj. Wen I last gon to Sankt Peterburg all the boyarz at the cort larfed at me. I giv the Tsar a Chineez ivery carvin wot I bort in Canton – one o them ball fingz full ov olez wiv anuver ball rattlin arand inside it an anuver ball in that an so on. Iz Madjisti was very perlite – eez a darmond geezer – but even so I dont fink e beleaved me izself.

Ope yur pub duz a rorin trade. Yu all diserv a rest after wot we bin fru. An best wishiz to evry one o yu.

Yur afekshunit frend

Kiril

We never even knew the Count's Christian name. He is called after St Cyril who, with St Methodius, brought Christianity to Russia, and also devised the Cyrillic alphabet in which Russian is written, which consists mainly of letters from St Cyril's native Greek with some additions from Coptic, or simply devised by the saint, to represent the sounds of a different language.

Like him, we have found that no one believes our tale, though they may be too polite to call us liars. No matter: we know what we have done. In the defiant words that Virgil put into the mouth of Aeneas, *Fuimus Troes; fuit Ilium, et ingens / Gloria Teucrorum* – We were Trojans; Troy was, and the great glory of the Trojans.

February 30ᵗʰ, 1812.

News has reached us that our old friend Sir Arthur Wellesley – or Wellington as I should now call him – has been advanced to the rank of Earl. We are only seven miles to the north-east of the village of Wellington from which he took his title. I had long been puzzled by this choice of name, but have now found that his brother Richard, the Earl of Mornington, chose it for him while Sir Arthur was busy fighting in Spain. There were two reasons for the choice: there happened to be a manor in the parish of Wellington for sale, which could be bought to provide a local attachment for the title; and the name sounded somewhat like Wellesley.

Thus great names are conferred by accident. I am told that the Duke of Devonshire, who resides in Derbyshire, traces his title to the illegible writing of a clerk in 1618 when his ancestor William Cavendish was due to be made Earl of Derbyshire by King James the First. And did not that great man Marcus Tullius Cicero inherit his cognomen from an ancestor who had a cleft tip to his nose that supposedly looked like a chickpea, *cicer*?

Wellington was rewarded with his new title after his victory at Salamanca, followed by the liberation of Madrid from the yoke of the Corsican tyrant. How I wish I had been there with the bears putting the French cavalry to rout as we did at Sahagún and Grijó! I do not think he will be greatly affected by the honour, for he is a practical soldier devoted to winning battles rather than honours. Nevertheless, if he survives this war – and, having saved his life once, I pray he will – I expect he will emerge from it as a victorious Duke.

To return to more humble matters, our inn continues to prosper. We have set up a small stage in the corner of the inn yard where it does not hinder our coaches from turning, and our nightly performances are famous in the locality and have attracted visitors from as far away as Bristol. Jem, with the aid of a local blacksmith and wheelwright, has constructed a new Unirota for Henry – no longer 'Little Henry' for he is is now as large as any of the bears and had long ago outgrown the original vehicle. He can now juggle seven balls while riding it around the yard, and is practising the juggling of flaming torches, which will be a brave spectacle when we perform after dark in winter. He often rides down the steep slope of Golden Hill at breakneck speed, to the amusement of the ladies of easy virtue whose establishments line the street.

Bruin and I have taught all the other bears to read and write reasonably well, which makes it easier for us to serve customers (at least, those who are literate) while we are not performing. Our existing servants were too few to cope with the increased business at the inn, and now it is all hands to the pumps (a metaphor all too real to us when the *Dronning Bengjerd* sprang a leak in the distant ocean).

May 15th, 1812.

Melancholy news: the miserable John Bellingham, whom we befriended in Archangel and found a ship to take him home, has shot and killed our Prime Minister Spencer Percival. How can a well intentioned deed have such evil results? I wish we had left the querulous wretch to rot on the quayside.

Perceval had been a stout defender of Wellington's campaign in Spain, while weaker voices in Parliament were demanding his recall. It is some consolation that his successor, Lord Liverpool, is of a mind to pursue the same policy. The bravest of soldiers is ever at risk from craven politicians.

To return to more cheerful matters, our two cubs Arthur and Rick (as we call little Frederick, to avoid confusing him with Fred) are now gambolling around to everyone's delight, including that of the visitors to the inn. We are well liked locally after we made a solemn pact with all the local farmers that we would never take any of their cattle, sheep, pigs, hens or other livestock, in a document to which each of the bears added his or her signature. This gives us the free run of the surrounding farmland, which we relieve of its teeming rabbits, foxes and badgers. Of course no one mentions the landowners' deer, either ourselves or the local poachers, but we are all privately partial to a morsel of venison.

July 6ᵗʰ, 1812.

My prediction to the Tsar has come true: Napoleon has invaded Russia. It is reported that he crossed the river Neman, which marks the frontier, on June 24th. I believe and hope that the remainder of my forecasting will be accurate: that he will advance until his troops, their lines of supply extended beyond feasibility, perish in the grip of the Russian winter. It does not matter how many battles he wins before this.

What a foolish little man the Corsican tyrant is! His army is already falling back in Spain thanks to Lord Wellington, and a prudent ruler would take that as a sign that he has expanded his empire as far as is practical. Yet now his devouring ambition has driven him to take on an insuperable enemy. We shall be rid of him in a few years, a cheering thought.

August 7th, 1812.

An alarming encounter this evening: the audience for our performance included none other than His Honour Mr Justice Isaiah Gaunt, who had presided over the infamous trial of Fred and had the unhappy task of sentencing him to death after the bribed jury returned their unreasonable verdict. We were unaware of his presence until after we had finished; luckily Jem and Dolores had been the only humans on stage while Fred, unrecognisable behind his beard, had been serving patrons behind the bar.

He accosted us genially, though we were quaking with fear, and expressed the wish that we were doing well. Jem took the bull by the horns, as he had to, and told him that Fred had escaped on a ship bound for Russia – which was the truth though not, as the judge would have had it, the whole truth. We were not on oath.

'Indeed, I am most glad to hear that,' said the judge. 'I knew, and everyone in the court knew, that the verdict was unjust, yet I was obliged to sentence him as I did, and it weighed heavily on my conscience. But when Mr Rowland so unexpectedly escaped from Newgate, I laughed aloud with huge relief. The old Nithsdale trick worked again, and immaculately carried out! The two gaolers were dismissed for drunkenness on duty, but that was no great loss.'

He was, he said, on his way to the assizes in Truro, but had left his party to see if the company of bears was the one he remembered. It was bound to happen sooner or later.

Taking a further chance, Jem enquired what might happen should Fred return to England. I think the judge knew that he already had, but what is not said is not heard. He replied, 'You should know that the woman calling herself Hesperia Fairbrother, who was the chief witness at the trial' – we all shivered, remembering her baleful testimony – 'was convicted last year on three counts of perjury and one of fraud. It seems that she had been on hire as a witness to anything, and the fraud concerned the sale of shares of a company pretending to have found gold in Wales. Her real name is Jane Scraggs, and it is under that name that she was transported to Australia along with the luckless men and women sent to colonise that barren shore.'

He went on, 'I can say to you now that, should Mr Rowland return, no action will be taken against him. Most fortunately no one was injured in the escape' – the glint in his eye showed that he knew we had had a part in it – 'and it would not, as they say, be in the public interest to pursue the matter further. As long as Mr Rowland does not put on a dramatic performance of how he escaped the law' – at this last word he made a little grimace of distaste – 'he will be as safe as anyone can be in this transitory world.'

We plied him with friendship and contraband brandy, and he returned to his party merrily, but not as merry as ourselves.

Our last obstacle to happiness has been removed, and we are content to live out our days in the peace and beauty of Somerset. No one can claim that they are truly fortunate: as Sophocles put it,

Οὐ χρή ποτ' εὖ πράσσοντος ὀλβίσαι τύχας
ἀνδρός, πρὶν αὐτῷ παντελῶς ἤδη βίος
διεκπεραθῇ καὶ τελευτήσῃ δρόμον.

Think not that fate has granted any man
Good fortune, till his life on earth has reached
Its full span, and his time draws to a close.

But we shall try.